## THORNE TAKES CHARGE

"Sergeant Abbot!" Thorne said.

"Yes, sir!"

"Get hold of John Kempton and tell him we'll need a room for interviews. Make sure everything is laid on. Direct external phone line as soon as possible. And other amenities. You know. I'm certain Kempton doesn't want an incident van parked in the front yard of the hotel."

"I understand, sir."

"Then I'll want a complete list of staff and guests. No one's to leave until they've been interviewed. If anyone screams, refer them to me. We'll start with the Ravens. And after them, John Kempton."

One of the detective-constables came up and spoke to his Inspector.

"Yes?" said Thorne quickly. "What is it?"

"They may have found the murder weapon, sir," said the Inspector, "and possibly the place where the deceased was killed."

"Show me." Thorne looked at the constable's trousers. "It's wet in there?"

"From yesterday's rain. Would you like a raincoat, sir?"

"No, thanks." Thorne was wearing one of his better suits today and the thought of what Miranda would say if he returned home with dirty trouser-legs flashed through his mind and made him more abrupt than he intended. "Well, come on then, man. Where is it?"

Bantam Books offers the finest in classic and modern English murder mysteries.
Ask your bookseller for the books you have missed.

## Agatha Christie

Death on the Nile
A Holiday for Murder
The Mousetrap and Other Plays
The Mysterious Affair at Styles
Poirot Investigates
Postern of Fate
The Secret Adversary
The Seven Dials Mystery
Sleeping Murder

## Patricia Wentworth

The Ivory Dagger
Miss Silver Comes to Stay
Poison in the Pen
She Came Back
Through the Wall

## Margery Allingham

Black Plumes
Dancers in Mourning
Deadly Duo
Death of a Ghost
The Fashion in Shrouds
Flowers for the Judge
Pearls Before Swine

## Dorothy Simpson

Close Her Eyes
Last Seen Alive
The Night She Died
Puppet for a Corpse
Six Feet Under

## John Greenwood

The Missing Mr. Mosely
Murder by Moonlight
Murder, Mr. Mosely

## Catherine Aird

Harm's Way
Henrietta Who?
His Burial Too
Last Respects
Parting Breath
Slight Mourning

## Elizabeth Daly

The Book of the Lion
Unexpected Night

## Anne Morice

Murder in Outline
Murder Post-Dated
Scared to Death
Sleep of Death

## John Penn

An Ad for Murder
A Deadly Sickness
Mortal Term
Stag Dinner Death
A Will to Kill

## Ruth Rendell

The Face of Trespass
The Lake of Darkness
No More Dying Then
Shake Hands Forever
A Sleeping Life
A Dark-Adapted Eye (writing as Barbara Vine)

## P. C. Doherty

Death of a King

## Aaron J. Elkins

Murder in the Queen's Armes

# UNTO
# THE
# GRAVE

## John Penn

BANTAM BOOKS
TORONTO · NEW YORK · LONDON · SYDNEY · AUCKLAND

This book is fiction. All the characters and
incidents in it are imaginary.

*This low-priced Bantam Book
has been completely reset in a type face
designed for easy reading, and was printed
from new plates. It contains the complete
text of the original hard-cover edition.*
NOT ONE WORD HAS BEEN OMITTED.

UNTO THE GRAVE
*A Bantam Book / published by arrangement with
William Collins Sons & Co., Ltd.*

PRINTING HISTORY
*Collins edition published in 1986
Bantam edition / March 1987*

ISBN 0-553-26454-0

*Published simultaneously in the United States and Canada*

PRINTED IN THE UNITED STATES OF AMERICA

O   0  9  8  7  6  5  4  3  2  1

# UNTO
# THE
# GRAVE

# Chapter 1

The Wychwood House Hotel lay in a fold of the Cotswold hills seven or eight miles north-east of Colombury and about three-quarters of an hour's drive from Oxford. It was a long, low building of local stone, set in some acres of land, and originally intended as a private dwelling. But the additions which had been necessary to turn it into a hotel had been cleverly planned and had mellowed over the years, so that now they were almost indistinguishable from the original structure.

Inside, the reception rooms were varied and spacious and comfortable. The bedrooms—eighteen double and two single, plus a couple of suites, one of them a so-called bridal suite—were modern, but extremely attractive, and naturally they all had their own bathroom, television sets, direct-line phones. There were flowers everywhere, supplemented in winter by arrangements of dried leaves and berries. The pictures on the walls were good prints, and there were occasional pieces of genuinely antique furniture that John Kempton and his wife, Rose, the owners, had picked up in sales and refurbished.

Given all this—an ideal setting, extensive grounds, luxurious surroundings, excellent service and wonderful food—the guests were fortunate. They were also rich. Their bills were large, but there were few complaints. The guests—visitors as the Kemptons preferred to call them—got what they demanded, and paid for it, plus a degree of personal consideration from the Kemptons that was beyond price.

1

It was twenty-odd years ago since the Kemptons had begun their married life managing a London pub. They were ambitious and they knew they were capable of a good deal more; after all, John had been properly trained as a hotelier, partly abroad. And when their son, Paul, began to toddle, they knew they had to make a change; a pub wasn't the best environment in which to bring up a young boy. It was then, when they were wondering how to set about achieving their aims, that they had a tremendous stroke of luck. John's aunt died suddenly and left him a surprisingly large sum. With what they'd saved they had been able to look around.

They finally lit upon the Wychwood House Hotel. The place had been badly run down, but together they had built it up. It was small, but that was how they liked it, and they had no intention of expanding very much further. They had done their best to blend modern amenities with old-fashioned comfort so as to create the atmosphere of a country house, and they'd succeeded admirably, helped by a fine chef. The Kemptons hoped that sometime in the distant future Paul would take over the business; he had shown every interest, been trained for the hotel trade and was beginning to be of considerable assistance to his parents. In the meantime, Wychwood House provided a comfortable and pleasant livelihood for the three of them.

It was a near-perfect mid-September Saturday, the pale sky hazy with sunshine and the weather wonderfully warm, when Detective-Superintendent George Thorne of the Thames Valley Police drove his wife, Miranda, from Kidlington to the Wychwood House Hotel for lunch, to fulfil a long-delayed engagement. The Thornes had known the Kemptons in London, for their pub had been George Thorne's local. The families had completely lost touch when the Kemptons left London, and it was not until Thorne was promoted and posted to Kidlington that they had all met by chance in Oxford, and been delighted to see each other again.

That was more than a year ago. Since then the Kemptons had spent a Sunday with the Thornes, but the

Thornes had never managed to visit the hotel. The demands on a senior police officer—especially an officer of the Serious Crime Squad—were always apt to disrupt his social life, but finally the Superintendent and his wife had been able to accept an invitation to lunch, without having to cancel the date at the last moment.

"It's quite a place!" Miranda Thorne exclaimed as they turned into the discreetly sign-posted tree-lined drive, and the house came into view. She patted her dark curly hair. Conscious of looking her best in a bright yellow suit—she loved bright colours—she was all ready to enjoy herself.

Thorne smiled at her fondly. He was neat and trim, more like an army officer than a policeman, and he knew that the vivacious Miranda seemed to many an unexpected wife for him. But he was devoted to her.

"Here we are," he said, as they were flagged down by a tall young man in dark green slacks and sweater. He brought the car to a halt and lowered the window. The man smiled pleasantly.

"Welcome to Wychwood House, sir. Do you know the way? If you care to leave your car at the entrance, I'll park it for you. We like to keep the driveway clear."

"What a well-spoken attractive young man," Miranda said.

"Yes," said Thorne absently. "And I've got a feeling I've seen him before somewhere." The Superintendent had an excellent memory for faces, though at the moment it had failed him. He made a mental note to ask Kempton for the name if he got the chance, then dismissed the subject from his mind.

The Kemptons were waiting to greet them in the hall. John was a big man, shrewd but friendly, in many ways a typical innkeeper, and Rose, fair, pretty, plumper than she had been, was a warm, outgoing woman. Miranda Thorne looked round appraisingly. "What a wonderful atmosphere!" she exclaimed at once.

"First impressions are very important in the hotel trade," Rose Kempton said. "This is meant to look like a private house when you enter. The reception desk is hidden at the back. You must meet Helen Dearden. She's the receptionist, and a good friend."

As Rose was speaking the front door opened and a couple came in. They were tall, slim, fair and were dressed identically in jeans and T-shirts. They could have been teen-age twins.

"Hi, Mrs. Kempton," they chorused in unison.

"Hello there," Rose said, smiling, and in response to Miranda's unspoken question added softly as the couple went to the lift. "Vern and Polly Raven from Boston, Massachusetts. They're newly-weds, in Europe for the first time on a honeymoon trip. His daddy gave it to them as a wedding present."

"Not your usual kind of guest, I imagine," Thorne remarked.

"No, indeed." Rose was amused. "Much younger than the average. But they're perfectly sweet. They go everywhere hand in hand."

"Come into the lounge and have a drink," said John at once. "We make a point of showing our faces in the bar and the lounges, especially before and after lunch. The visitors seem to like it. It gives them a chance to air any complaints," he added.

"And it's all part of the family atmosphere we try to cultivate," Rose said. "We'll have lunch in our own apartment, of course, and after coffee we'll show you round the place. How's that for a programme?"

"It sounds wonderful," said Miranda.

John Kempton turned as a figure emerged from the rear premises. "You remember Paul?" he said. "He's just twenty-one." The resemblance between father and son was immediately apparent.

"Frankly, no," laughed Thorne. "The last time I saw you, Paul, you were a snotty-nosed kid in short trousers." Paul laughed in his turn as John ushered the party to a corner of a large and pleasant lounge. It was clear, as John Kempton had said, that the guests in the lounge were quite accustomed to the hotelier and his wife joining them for drinks, and a number of hands were raised in greeting.

"So, how's business?" Thorne asked casually as he sipped his whisky and soda.

"Flourishing," said John Kempton. "To use the jargon of the trade, we've got a growing up-market reputation and a regular clientèle we can depend on. We've had some complimentary mentions in good food guides and things like that—"

"Largely thanks to Felix," Rose put in.

"Felix?" queried Miranda.

"Our chef. He's French. Monsieur Lechat. It's spelt as one word but with a name like that what else could we call him? I don't think he'd have liked 'Puss.' He's a fierce little man sometimes."

"And all without advertising," went on John Kempton. "Though there was a useful article in an American airline magazine that led to a lot of visitors from overseas. And Coriston College is only a few miles away, so we get quite a few parents staying here. There's a couple of them over there," he added quietly, nodding towards another corner of the room. "A Major Winston and his wife, Lady Georgina. They've got two boys at 'Corston,' as they call it. She's a bit of a pain sometimes, but they're regulars."

At that point a couple came into the lounge, and greeted the Kemptons. John grinned welcomingly. "Hello, Mr. Fowler, Mrs. Fowler. You must meet our friends from Kidlington. Superintendent George Thorne, and his wife, Miranda."

The Fowlers were a small couple, so similar in appearance that they could easily have been taken for brother and sister rather than husband and wife. They were obviously in their middle sixties and their once red hair had faded, but their eyes were still blue and quick with intelligent interest. They had no hesitation in taking the chairs which John Kempton pulled up, and it was soon apparent that originally they came from Scotland.

"Anne and I were the Kemptons' very first guests," said William Fowler proudly, "and we've been coming back to Wychwood House every year since."

"We consider the Kemptons as dear friends by this time," Anne Fowler added. "And, of course, it's a wonderful hotel. We recommend it to all our friends."

Thorne rather liked the Fowlers. "How did you hear

about it in the first place?" he asked. "It's a long way from Scotland."

"A colleague in Colombury told me about it," Fowler said. "I was a solicitor before I retired. My firm—I practised in London—had some dealings there."

Rose Kempton and Mrs. Fowler had been speaking quietly together, and they looked up as the others stopped talking. "Mr. and Mrs. Fowler are going to have a party to celebrate their fortieth wedding anniversary while they're here this year," Rose explained. "We were just discussing some of the arrangements."

As they had promised, the Kemptons took the Thornes away to lunch in their own private quarters, though the extensive menu was identical with that served to the guests. The food fully justified Felix's reputation, and the Superintendent, who was fond of his meals, finally sank back, replete. "That was wonderful," he said. "I'm not surprised you're making such a success of this place."

"It's been a lot of work," said Kempton, "hard work, and a lot of luxuries done without. I couldn't have managed it without Rose. She's been a tower of strength. But things are getting a little easier now Paul's finished his training and can help."

"Let's go back to the lounge for coffee," Rose said, "before we tour Wychwood House."

"Fine," said Thorne. "Why not?"

The four of them were followed into the lounge by another pair of guests—a woman of "uncertain age," with white hair, but an unlined, pretty if petulant face, and an attentive husband. Even on such a warm day the woman had a mink cape round her shoulders as if she were cold. Though she didn't look noticeably unhealthy, the cape gave her the air of an invalid.

The woman glanced inquiringly at the Thornes. "You're new guests," she said somewhat accusingly.

Explanations followed, and with some slight reluctance Rose Kempton invited the couple to join them. Their name turned out to be Blair, and they tended to dominate the conversation, describing their latest cruise.

"We love the Far East," Maurice Blair said. "We always feel at home there. A bit different from Maidenhead, where we live now." He was in his forties, a short stiff-backed man with a pleasant, friendly face. "Nina spent most of her childhood east of Suez."

"My father was a diplomat," Mrs. Blair explained.

It was not a conversation to which any of the others could contribute much. Miranda tried to comment on the luncheon food, but Mrs. Blair promptly criticized it. "I like highly spiced things," she said. "When we were in Singapore . . ."

Later, when they had made excuses and escaped to the hall, John Kempton apologized. "Sorry about that," he said. "Blair's a nice enough fellow, but she's a menace. She's not a well woman, of course, but she takes pretty good care of herself as far as I can see. Now, let's set off."

The Superintendent stroked his neat military moustache, and John Kempton, taking the gesture to express a lack of interest in the interior of the hotel, said, "Rose, why don't you show Miranda some of the rooms, while George and I have a stroll in the grounds."

Miranda got to her feet and followed Rose willingly. Her interest was merely casual, but she was fully prepared to be interested and to admire. Rose, she knew, was proud of the place.

At the reception desk Rose introduced Helen Dearden, a woman about her own age with a pleasant face and an efficient manner. As receptionist, Mrs. Dearden explained, she dealt with all the bookings and coped with innumerable other tasks.

"We don't have a proper concierge," she said. "One wouldn't really fit in. So I look after all the problems, the unforeseen things that crop up, even in the best of hotels." She smiled at Miranda, but suddenly became serious. "Which reminds me. If you could spare me a moment, Rose . . ."

It was clear that she wanted to discuss some private matter, and Miranda wandered tactfully away. She looked at the hunting prints in the hall and, when Rose still didn't reappear, went into a room that was obviously a small lounge. It was unoccupied except for a small, grey-haired lady who glanced up at her inquiringly.

"I'm sorry," Miranda apologized automatically. "I didn't

mean to disturb you." She stopped abruptly. "You're Cassandra Gray!" she said. "I've seen you on television and I've read nearly all your books."

"I hope you enjoyed them." The voice was amused.

"I most certainly did. I love historical novels." Miranda had crossed to where Miss Gray was sitting and she could see the magazine on the writer's lap. She stared at it in surprise. "Miss Gray, you're doing an acrostic," she said.

"I often do. They stimulate the mind and relax one at the same time. Do you do them?"

"I make them up," Miranda said. "And that's one of mine. I recognize it."

"Fascinating. Then you can tell me—"

Miranda was never to know what Cassandra Gray wanted to ask. There was a muffled thump behind her and a low moan. Miranda swung round. Rose Kempton had entered the room silently and was leaning against the wall by the door. She was breathing heavily, her chest rising and falling rapidly, while one hand groped behind her as if for support. Miranda ran to her and helped her into a chair. She was pale and there was a film of sweat on her upper lip.

"I'll get John," Miranda said. "Miss Gray, will you—"

"No! Please, no," Rose interrupted. "I'm all right. I don't want any fuss. It was just—I felt faint suddenly." She spoke haltingly and her mouth twisted into a grimace. "It's just that—that I didn't sleep too well last night."

Miranda hesitated, but already Rose's breathing had eased and a little colour was returning to her cheeks. Miranda looked at her in some doubt, but Cassandra Gray nodded reassuringly.

"Rest for a moment or two, Mrs. Kempton," Miss Gray said. "Would you like a glass of water?"

"No, thanks." Rose shook her head. She was recovering quickly now. "I'm sorry to have made such an exhibition of myself. Please forget it, will you, Miss Gray—Miranda?"

This time Rose's facial muscles managed a genuine smile, and she got to her feet. She seemed quite steady. Cassandra Gray nodded again, glanced at Miranda and returned to her acrostic. Miranda went with Rose. She was worried, but it wasn't her business and clearly Rose wanted the episode unmentioned. In any case, she seemed reasonably normal as she showed Miranda around the kitchens and some of the bedrooms.

Half an hour later the Thornes said their goodbyes in the hall, while their car was fetched.

"A very, very good lunch, and pleasant company," George Thorne said, pronouncing his verdict as they moved off down the drive.

"It was lovely," Miranda agreed, her brown eyes sparkling.

The attractive young man in green slacks and sweater who had parked their car was ready to direct them. "Damn," said Thorne. "I meant to find out who that chap was."

"His name's Tom Latimer," Miranda said. "I asked Rose. She says he's a sort of odd job man, and very good at his odd jobs. He's not a local. He comes from London."

"Is that so?" said Thorne. "Interesting. His name means nothing to me, but I'd swear we've met before somewhere." He brooded on the problem for much of the journey home.

Passing through the hall later in the afternoon, Rose found her husband in conversation with Helen Dearden at the reception desk. He looked up sharply as she approached and said, "Rose, you never mentioned that the Cunninghams had cancelled, and that a man called Roy Mortlake—a new visitor—phoned and took their room."

Rose paused before she answered. "No, I'm sorry. Helen told me just after lunch, and I forgot, what with the Thornes—"

"I see." John Kempton paused also. "Anyway, he's just phoned again. He's been delayed for some reason and he won't be arriving till this evening."

"In time for dinner?" Rose's voice was level.

"Around six." Kempton was equally casual.

"Fine." Abruptly Rose walked away. "I'll go and check his room," she said.

Kempton watched her, his mouth set in grim lines. Then, with a nod at Helen, who was wondering if the

Kemptons had had a quarrel, he went through to the office where most of the hotel's paperwork was dealt with. But he was restless and he couldn't settle.

Mortlake, he thought. The name had come as a shock to him. It wasn't a "Smith, Brown or Jones" kind of name. And the first name, Roy, as well as Rose's odd manner, made it more than possible that this was the bloody bastard she had known years ago before she had become Mrs. Kempton.

Rose herself had never mentioned the man's surname; she had merely called him Roy. But Kempton, helping to pack for their move to Wychwood House, had come on a snap with a name on it that had fallen from the back of a photo frame. Taking his cue from Rose, he had never sought to embarrass her by referring to the incident and, as far as he knew, Rose had no idea that the name Mortlake might mean something to him. John Kempton sighed; unless the man had changed a great deal over the years, he'd soon know.

Roy Mortlake arrived at Wychwood House shortly after six o'clock. He had come by train to Colombury, and thence by taxi. "A tiring journey for a man not long out of hospital," he said.

John Kempton, in spite of his inner feelings, was profuse in his apologies. "My dear sir, if you'd let us know we'd have sent a car to meet you. You never mentioned you'd been ill, and we assumed you'd be driving yourself."

"Just a minor operation. Nothing serious; nothing that a couple of weeks' rest in your establishment won't set right." Mortlake brushed aside Kempton's apologies.

The years had changed Roy Mortlake, but he was recognizably an older version of the man in Rose's snapshot. He was still big, with thick brown hair, a heavy moustache and a florid complexion. He didn't look as if he'd had a day's illness in his life. Certainly his operation hadn't made him lose weight, though his impeccably tailored suit hid his size, and went well with the silk shirt, Dior tie and handmade shoes. An opulent man and full of confidence, Kempton thought. He had taken an instant dislike to Mortlake.

Rose appeared as Roy Mortlake was signing the register. Normally she wore little make-up, but this evening was clearly an exception. And Kempton guessed from the brightness of her eyes that she'd already had at least one strong drink. John had no option but to introduce her.

"Mr. Mortlake, this is my wife."

"Good evening, Mr. Mortlake. Welcome to our house." Rose didn't offer her hand.

" 'Evening, Mrs. Kempton."

For a moment a shadow seemed to pass across Roy Mortlake's face. Then it was gone, leaving only a tiny frown as he returned his attention to the register. He took his time about it. The Kemptons waited as Tom Latimer brought in the bags.

Rose said, "I've one or two things to do. Will you look after Mr. Mortlake, John?"

"Of course, Rose."

Kempton hadn't taken his eyes off Mortlake, and as he casually spoke Rose's name, he saw Mortlake's hand become still. He felt physically sick. There was no doubt.

But if this was true, there were many unanswered questions. Was it chance that had brought Mortlake to Wychwood House, or had he deliberately sought out Rose? And if his visit was deliberate, why had he come? What was his purpose? I'll kill him before I let him harm her, Kempton thought, and was shocked by the violence of his feelings.

# Chapter 2

John Kempton looked doubtfully at his wife across the breakfast table. He knew she'd slept badly the last two nights for he'd heard her get up frequently, and there had been occasional sounds from the bathroom as if she were attempting to vomit. When eventually she came back to bed she tossed and turned. The previous day, Sunday, she had been tense and *distraite* and now, if anything, she seemed more on edge, snapping at him unnecessarily over trifles.

Kempton sighed. Normally Rose had an even temper; she was rarely irritable, and had no hesitation in admitting that she felt unwell. He yearned to comfort her, to tell her that he knew the cause of her anxiety, but it was so obvious that she didn't want his assistance that, coward-like, he couldn't bring himself to mention Roy Mortlake.

"I'm going to check on the wines," he said finally, noting that Rose had eaten very little. "I know we're getting low on the Chablis, and I must make sure we have enough of the claret the old Canon likes. You've remembered the Hurleys are arriving this morning?"

"Yes, of course I've remembered. Their letter said eleven o'clock, and that's when they'll be here. The Canon believes in punctuality." Rose was tart. "You needn't worry; I'll be ready to greet them. Meanwhile I'm off to discuss the Fowlers' party with Felix."

"Fine! See you later, love."

John smiled at Rose warmly, but Rose was turning away, her thoughts clearly elsewhere. But whether she

was merely intent on her immediate task, or whether she
was intentionally avoiding further discussion, John had no
means of knowing. In fact, Rose was busying herself about
the hotel in an effort not to think at all.

She found plenty to occupy her in the kitchen. Monsieur Lechat was in a rage. He was standing in the middle
of his domain, brandishing a large knife and swearing
volubly in French. Luckily those of his staff who hadn't
made themselves scarce understood very little of it.

"What on earth's the matter, Felix?" Rose exclaimed.

"I am leaving. Now. At once. That woman, she is
*impossible*. Either she go or I go!"

"I don't know who you're talking about, Felix, but
whoever she is I'd rather lose her than you," Rose said
soothingly. "Tell me."

"That Mrs. Blair. She knows I do not make the hot
Indian curry, only the cool Indonesian. Much better for
the inside. Why does she take curry last night, and then
complain? There was plenty of choice. She could have . . ."
Felix continued in this vein for some time.

"She came in here and complained to you personally?"
Rose was astounded and annoyed. "I'm sorry, Felix. She
had no right to do that. It won't happen again, I promise. Any
messages from the visitors—compliments or otherwise—they
should come through me or Mr. Kempton. You know that."

"We-ell, as long as we understand each other, Mrs.
Kempton." The little Frenchman's temper subsided as
quickly as it had arisen. "But you must tell the woman
that I will never—never—have her in my kitchens."

"Yes, yes," said Rose, who was not unused to tan-
trums of this kind. "I will, Felix. Now, let's go into your
office and discuss what you're going to do for Mr. and Mrs.
Fowler's anniversary. I'd like it to be especially nice for
them. They don't want a cake, but . . ."

Half an hour later Rose emerged from the little room
that had once been the butler's pantry, but was now
Monsieur Lechat's private office. The chef, who knew the
Fowlers well and liked them, was fully prepared to extend
himself on their behalf. Rose was more than satisfied with
his suggestions, and indeed with Felix himself. He could
be very temperamental, but he was irreplaceable. He had

done a great deal to enhance the hotel's reputation, and it was unthinkable that Nina Blair should upset him. Silently she cursed Mrs. Blair.

Almost immediately she met Maurice Blair in the hall, and expressed her feelings with some force. Blair was nonplussed. He knew his wife made a fuss about her food, but he had thought this was a quirk the Kemptons accepted. He stammered his apologies.

"I'm dreadfully sorry, Mrs. Kempton, but—" He stopped. He wasn't prepared to say anything against Nina. He began again. "My wife is a sick woman, as you're aware, Mrs. Kempton, and that makes her more—more particular."

"Maybe, but I can't have my chef upset in this way. If Mrs. Blair isn't satisfied with our food or service, I suggest she—"

"Mrs. Kempton, you're not asking us to leave? Please!" Blair was plainly aghast. "We've been coming here for five years now, and I can't think what—what we'd do. We'd never find anywhere else so—so suitable—so comfortable— where we'd be shown so much consideration."

Rose, who had been carried away by her own rhetoric and had no intention of asking the Blairs to go, was in her turn surprised by Maurice Blair's vehemence. She hadn't meant to be unpleasant. In normal circumstances she tolerated Nina Blair, and she liked Maurice as a pleasant easy-going character. But today—today was different. Hastily she collected her thoughts.

"Of course I don't want you to leave, Mr. Blair," Rose said. Impulsively she patted him on the arm. "Just have a word with your wife, will you? If there's anything she dislikes let me know, but don't go upsetting Felix. Think of the food without him!" She smiled.

"Thank you." Blair showed his relief. "You're very kind, Mrs. Kempton. If I may make a personal remark, Wychwood House wouldn't be the same without you. We both hope you never have any reason to leave."

"Thank you."

But Rose's friendly expression had faded. She nodded and, turning away abruptly, went to speak to Helen Dearden at the reception desk. Maurice Blair looked after her, puzzled. He assumed that he had offended her in some way, but he couldn't think how.

He was standing there, feeling helpless, when the front door swung open and Lady Georgina Winston strode through the hall in the direction of the lift. Tall, athletic, she was normally attractive, but at the moment her mouth was set hard, there were spots of angry colour on her cheeks and she exuded fury. She ignored Maurice Blair's greeting completely.

Major Winston followed his wife. Derek Winston was fractionally shorter than Lady Georgina, but exceedingly handsome—so handsome that his looks alone might have made him a film star, even if his acting abilities were negligible. He glanced at Blair as he passed.

"Women!" he said. He grinned somewhat sheepishly as he hurried after Lady Georgina, but Maurice Blair felt little sympathy as he too went in search of his wife.

It was eleven o'clock and, as Rose had predicted, Canon Hurley's Daimler was arriving with its customary punctuality. The Canon and Mrs. Hurley sat in state in the back of the car, while their daughter, Alice, drove. Alice was a competent driver but today, for some reason, she braked so sharply when they reached the front door that she startled her parents.

"Really, Alice!" Canon Hurley expostulated. "That was careless of you. You might have hurt us."

Alice Hurley apologized a little breathlessly, her thoughts elsewhere. Awkwardly she climbed out of the driving seat. She could feel her heart bumping against her ribs. When her mother had been ill and there had been a possibility that their holiday would have to be cancelled she had been in despair, but now they had actually arrived she wished herself anywhere else.

Tom Latimer came running to help the Canon and Mrs. Hurley from the car.

"How nice to see you again, sir," he said, "and Mrs. Hurley and Miss Hurley."

"It's nice to be here, Latimer," Canon Hurley said. "Isn't it?" he added, looking around at the familiar façade and addressing his wife and daughter.

Margaret Hurley nodded her agreement, and gave the dry cough that had remained with her after her recent illness. Alice said nothing. She avoided Latimer's glance, and moved round to open the boot of the car.

"Here, let me, Miss Hurley."

At once Tom Latimer was beside her, bending over and lifting the heavy suitcases to the ground. His hand brushed against hers; it could have been either accidental or deliberate and she turned away from him. But her foot slipped and he caught her by the arm to steady her. He held her longer than was strictly necessary.

"Who," said Canon Hurley, "is that?"

Miss Gray was walking briskly up the drive. "That's Miss Cassandra Gray, sir," Latimer said. "A novelist of some repute, I believe."

The Canon made no comment. "And that extraordinary young couple?" He pointed to the backs of the Ravens who, both wearing very short shorts and holding hands, had jogged past the front of the hotel. "Are they staying here?"

"That's Mr. and Mrs. Raven, sir. From America." Latimer allowed himself an amused smile, directed at Alice. "They're on their honeymoon."

Canon Hurley grunted. He seemed to disapprove of the Ravens. "Well, let's get inside," he said, and added as Rose appeared in the doorway, "Ah, here's Mrs. Kempton to welcome us."

It took Rose fifteen minutes to ensconce the Hurleys in their adjoining rooms. She paid special attention to Alice, as always feeling a little sorry for the girl. Such a pity, she thought, that Alice had taken after her father rather than her pretty, if faded, mother. Nevertheless, the girl seemed to be making more effort over herself than she had in previous years; she really looked quite attractive this morning, Rose thought. But she didn't have to make such a fuss about a lost glove.

"It could easily be in the car," Rose agreed, suppressing her feelings. "We'll get—"

"Mother," Alice interrupted, abruptly leaving Rose and hurrying into the next room. "Mrs. Kempton thinks I've probably dropped my glove in the car. I'm just going down to see."

"All right, dear."

"But don't be long," the Canon said. "It'll soon be time for lunch."

"No, no, I'll be right back," Alice said quickly.

Rose spent a few more moments with the Hurleys, then went downstairs. Her husband was passing through the hall.

"Just going to inspect the gutter over the garages," he said, making a valiant attempt to sound normally cheerful. "Tom says we've got a leak." He waited, but Rose merely nodded.

John Kempton went out of a side door and round to the back of the house, where garages had been converted from the old stables—a large covered area and a couple of separate lock-ups.

His mind occupied with a variety of conflicting fears and doubts, he came unexpectedly on Alice Hurley and Tom Latimer. It was one of those embarrassing moments to which everyone is sometimes subject. He had the impression that he had interrupted something intimate—a kiss or an embrace?—but the idea was surely absurd, though the couple had certainly been standing very close together, and had drawn apart hastily.

Latimer was the first to regain his composure, if indeed he had ever lost it. He said, "Miss Hurley mislaid a glove and came to see if she'd left it in her car."

"And had you, Miss Hurley? Have you found it?" Kempton heard the unspoken suspicion in his voice, and regretted it. After all, the explanation of a lost glove was plausible. Too plausible? Why had Latimer offered it, and not the Hurley girl?

"Yes. Yes, thank you. I must have dropped it on the floor as I got out of the car." Alice smiled uneasily at John Kempton, and gave Latimer a brief nod. "Thank you," she repeated. "I'd better get ready for lunch."

There was a momentary silence as Alice left the two men. Then Tom Latimer said, "Now what can I do for you, sir?"

Kempton hesitated. It was not the words but the tone that had verged on insolence. Deliberately Kempton chose to ignore the challenge, if challenge it was; he wasn't in the mood for an argument that would probably turn out to be pointless. He said, "All right, Tom. What about this gutter that's supposed to be leaking?"

# Chapter 3

"Give you a yard's start and beat you to the other end," Vern Raven shouted.

His wife didn't bother to reply. She had already pushed herself off from the wall of the pool, and was swimming strongly. Vern took a running dive and was after her. They arrived, breathing hard and laughing, within a couple of seconds of each other. Both claimed victory.

"I won, didn't I?" Polly appealed to Major Winston, who was standing on the diving board.

"Of course, my dear!" Derek Winston eyed her appreciatively as she pulled herself out of the water. How was it, he wondered, that American girls managed to have those extraordinary boyish figures and still look sexy as hell. This one was a gem. He wouldn't mind having a go himself if . . .

"Nonsense!" Lady Georgina interrupted his thoughts, which she'd had no difficulty in guessing. "Mr. Raven won easily. Didn't he, Canon? Mrs. Hurley? Mrs. Blair?—but I don't think you or your husband could have seen from where you're sitting."

The pool, large and rectangular—not kidney-shaped or any other curious design—was an important part of the Wychwood House scene. It had been built close to the house, in what had once been an extensive kitchen garden, long neglected when the Kemptons took the place over. A paved terrace surrounded it and the traditional high wall, of Cotswold stone, protected it on three sides, that nearest to the house pierced by a path which ran

18

through an archway. Beside the archway a brightly coloured awning extended from the wall to cover an elegant marble counter or bar, on which a waiter was even now arranging bottles and glasses and china in preparation for pre-lunch poolside drinks or after-lunch coffee.

On the fourth side—that most distant from the house— the wall had been in too bad a state of repair and a shrubbery, now grown dense, had been planted among the trees that stood beyond. A narrow paved path wound through this shrubbery to more open grounds which also belonged to the hotel. There had been no need to construct dressing-rooms or showers by the pool, for visitors could change and bathe in the comfort of their hotel rooms. The pool was heated, of course, and the whole area was sheltered at any time of the year, and in fine weather was a perfect sun-trap.

This morning, in addition to the three or four people actually in the pool several of the hotel guests were taking their ease around it before lunch, relaxing on lounges to make the most of these last wonderful days that must represent the end of summer. Even Mrs. Blair, who always felt cold, was there, comfortably wrapped in a wool rug. Maurice Blair sat beside her, reading a book.

"Look at that girl!" Nina Blair said. "She might as well wear nothing as those two little bits of fabric."

Blair glanced up. "She's only a child," he said mildly. Polly Raven did nothing for him. He patted his wife on the knee. "She should have your figure, Nina."

Nina Blair smiled. She was indeed proud of her figure which, despite her inability to take strenuous exercise, had retained its trim shape. "The girl's a fool," she said. "She's asking for trouble, flaunting herself like that. Did you see the way Major Winston was looking at her?"

Blair grunted and returned to his book. Canon Hurley might have been more responsive; he had already expressed his disapproval of Polly Raven.

"You can't imagine Alice displaying herself like that, can you?" he had said to his wife, unaware of the expression that flitted across his daughter's face. "She'd be much too sensible."

Sensible, Alice Hurley thought. Sensible, that was

the adjective that suited her. Not attractive, not desirable, not even just pretty. And, unbelievably at twenty-four, still a virgin. Old-fashioned parents, a single-sex day school, a secretarial course while she continued to live at home, and after that—secretary to her father. Hardly a recipe for riotous living. Hardly a recipe for meeting men. No, till recently she'd not had much chance and she envied Polly Raven with all her heart.

"I'm a bit chilly," she said. "I'm going up to my room to get a cardigan." She smiled brightly at her parents, who glanced up in return. "I shan't be long," she said.

Alice hurried along the edge of the pool and through the stone archway, on to the path to the house. She was not in the least cold, but she'd had to find some excuse to get away. If she'd stayed she could easily have burst into tears—for reasons that would have been literally inexplicable to her parents. She collected her keys and went up to her room.

To her annoyance a chamber maid was making the bed. The girl had just started and would clearly be some time. Alice found a cardigan. As she was about to leave she heard the sound of a vacuum cleaner next door. She thought for a moment and then acted.

She swept along the corridor and into her parents' bedroom with an aplomb that was foreign to her. "I need to get something for my mother," she announced.

"What, miss?" The machine was switched off.

In the sudden silence Alice repeated herself, and this time the words sounded forced and stupid; after all, there was no reason why she shouldn't interrupt the girl. She went through the bedroom and the maid nodded her understanding, turning the vacuum cleaner on again. Alice was alone in her parents' bathroom.

Her mother's cough mixture was to one side of the washbasin, as she had expected. With a sweep of her hand she knocked it sideways, and watched with pleasure as the glass bottle shattered and the thick dark brown liquid gurgled slowly down the drain. She returned to the bedroom and, her colour high, gestured to the maid to turn off her cleaner.

"I'm awfully sorry," she said. "I've had an accident—

broken a bottle of medicine. Careless of me—but you'll clear it up, won't you?"

"Yes of course, miss."

"Thank you very much. I'll explain to my mother. Thank you."

Alice fled, unaware of the pitying glance the girl cast after her. Not that she would have cared. For once in her life she had taken some positive action, and she had no regrets, whatever the consequences.

Roy Mortlake punched the bell beside the bar. No one came. Apart from himself the lounge was empty. Angrily he went into the hall and approached the reception desk. It was Mrs. Dearden's day off, and Paul Kempton was on duty in her place.

"Isn't it possible to get a drink in this bloody place?" Mortlake demanded.

"Of course—sir. Whenever you wish," Paul said coldly; guests at Wychwood House didn't normally speak to the staff like that. He had to stop himself from looking pointedly at the clock, which showed just eleven-fifteen. "Isn't the barman there? He must have gone down to the cellar for a moment. What can I get you?"

"A gin and tonic. I'll be at the bar."

"Yes, sir. Right away."

"Thanks," Mortlake said a few minutes later, when Paul had served him his drink. "Tell me . . ."

He kept Paul talking, asking questions about the hotel. Did the Kemptons own it? Or merely manage it? Was it they who had extended it? And among such questions he slipped in more personal ones, which Paul saw no reason not to answer frankly. They amused him.

"He's a curious guy," Paul said to Tom Latimer, who was bringing in wood. "The things he asked! How old I was. Was I an only child? Maybe he just meant to be pleasant, but really . . ." Laughing, Paul shook his head.

He would have been less light-hearted if he could have read Roy Mortlake's thoughts at that moment. Mortlake's intention had been to acquire information, and what he had learnt pleased him. He decided he might stay longer at Wychwood House than the couple of weeks he had originally intended.

As he contemplated this idea, Rose came into the room. She was completing her daily round to check that everything was in order and she hadn't expected to find Mortlake in the lounge. So far she had managed to avoid being alone with him, and she would have left at once if he had not called to her.

"Mrs. Kempton!"

"Yes, Mr. Mortlake?" Rose turned slowly.

Roy Mortlake grinned at her. "You're not being very friendly, Rose. Don't tell me you've forgotten the one-time light of your life. I haven't changed that much. I'm still your dearly-beloved Roy. But you—yes, you've changed. I didn't recognize you at first. Then, when Kempton called you Rose, I knew. Different hairstyle, more weight, more—more self-assurance. Not at all the little waif I used to—"

"I'm sorry, Mr. Mortlake, but you've made a mistake. I'm not your—your friend, whoever she was." Rose spoke quickly, too quickly; her words carried no conviction.

Mortlake threw back his head and guffawed with laughter. "You're not the little rosebud I taught to bloom? Come off it, Rose. Of course you are. You know that as well as I do. I've been having a chat with that son of yours—"

"Leave him out of it!" Rose was shaking. "He's nothing to do with you! Nothing!"

"Of course not, Rose. Don't get excited. You've only got to look at him to see he's Kempton's son. A nice boy. And he's devoted to you." Mortlake's smile was broad.

"God!" Rose clenched her fists. She swallowed hard. She felt helpless, vulnerable, just as she had all those years ago. But now it was worse, much worse. There was Paul to consider, and John, of course. She knew how much they loved her—and how bitterly unhappy she could make them both.

"What do you want, Roy?" she said finally. "If it's money, you're out of luck. Everything we have is invested in Wychwood House. There's none to spare. You've wasted your time coming here."

Mortlake shook his head. "I doubt that, Mrs.—er—Kempton. Believe it or not, I haven't thought of you for ages. If I had, I wouldn't have expected to find you in such comfortable circumstances. However, one shouldn't look a gift hotel in the chef, as they say, so I'll have to give the matter a little thought and see what advantage I can get from it."

"For heaven's sake, Roy, haven't you done me enough harm? Can't you leave us alone? You've nothing to gain. Nothing!" Rose was near to tears. "Go! Please go!"

"You must be joking—Mrs. Kempton."

Mortlake added the name as there was a loud bang. Tom Latimer, carrying an armful of logs, was standing in the doorway. A log had rolled from the top of the pile and crashed to the floor.

"I'm sorry, Mrs. Kempton. Mr. Mortlake, sir, I apologize. That was careless of me, but the pile slipped. I shouldn't have tried to carry so many."

Latimer dumped the logs in the hearth and returned to collect the one he had dropped. There was no means of knowing how long he had been in the room, how much he had overheard. With total nonchalance, he proceeded to pile the logs in their basket at the side of the hearth.

When he got to his feet, his task completed, Mortlake had gone, but Rose was still there, fighting to control her distress. Latimer pretended not to notice.

"Seems silly to be bringing in wood in this lovely weather," he remarked casually, "but it could get suddenly nippy in the evenings, and then you'd be glad of a fire. Anyway, Mrs. Kempton, it'll dry better in here than outside."

His chatter gave Rose a chance to regain her composure. She straightened her shoulders and took a deep breath. "Very—very sensible of you, Tom," she said.

"Mr. Paul's idea, actually," Latimer replied laconically.

He let her precede him from the room, and thought what a kind and pleasant woman she was. He was grateful to her, and to John Kempton. He owed them both. They had taken him on trust—no references, no nothing—and had given him a job and a home and restored some of the self-pride he had lost. Without them he would have gone completely down the drain. Should it become necessary, he thought, he would do a great deal more for either of them than just let a log drop on the floor at the right moment.

"I can't think how you could have been so careless, Alice," Mrs Hurley said plaintively. "My medicine wasn't anywhere near the edge of the washbasin. And anyway, why were you in our bathroom?"

"I told you. The maid was there and the door was open and I was looking for an aspirin, Mother," Alice lied glibly. "I had the beginnings of a headache."

It was after lunch. The Hurleys were having coffee in one of the smaller lounges. They were alone, except for Cassandra Gray, seemingly deep in a bird book, and Roy Mortlake, buried behind a newspaper.

The Canon said, "Well, no great harm done, Alice. But you'll have to go into Colombury and find a chemist. I was hoping you and I could have a short walk together this afternoon."

"You know how your father likes a companion on his walks," Margaret Hurley said, "and I'm not up to it yet."

Alice bit the inside of her lip and forced herself to smile ingratiatingly. She didn't care a damn, but some response was needed. "Perhaps if someone else is going . . ." She glanced at the newspaper that shielded Mortlake, and caught Miss Gray's eye.

Cassandra Gray gave an almost imperceptible shake of her head. She wasn't a selfish woman. She was certainly going for a walk and another day, if only for Alice's sake, she would have gladly agreed to Canon Hurley's company. But she was having difficulties with her current manuscript. She needed to be alone. The bird book and the small field glasses that were always with her were mainly camouflage. True, she would probably make use of them, but today her main purpose was to think about her characters and try to resolve her problem.

Roy Mortlake seemed to feel that eyes were turning to him. He lowered his newspaper. "Sorry," he said. "I've had my exercise for today. I prefer the early mornings when it's possible."

"Maybe Mr. Blair . . ." Cassandra Gray said, as Maurice Blair glanced into the room. "Mr. Blair often takes what he calls a constitutional in the afternoons, he told me. Don't you, Mr. Blair?" she added more loudly.

"What's that? Did I hear my name?"

There was a certain amount of light banter, and in the end all agreed that the Canon and Maurice Blair should walk together, while their wives rested. Relieved, Alice Hurley left them discussing whether to go by the lanes to Fairford village or to cut through the grounds of Wychwood House to the woods beyond. She didn't care. She had escaped.

The Hurleys' staid Daimler was not the most suitable of cars for the narrow winding roads that led from the hotel to Colombury. Nor did it suit Alice's mood—a fast convertible with the top down might have done that. But she opened both front windows and let the warm breeze blow through her hair. She felt happy and excited. She was wearing a new two-piece that she had bought especially for the holiday, and she hoped she looked her best.

Driving quickly, Alice reached Colombury quite soon, but she had difficulty finding somewhere to park. The little market town seemed to be full of people, so many of them strolling in the road that she had to concentrate on avoiding them and could scarcely search for a place to leave the car. Finally she abandoned it in a side street under a "No Parking" sign and half ran to the Windrush Arms.

She wasn't late. No specific time had been agreed. All Tom Latimer had said was that he had to go to Colombury that afternoon to collect some things for Mrs. Kempton, and if she could be in the Windrush about three-thirty, he would buy her a cup of tea. But now, as she hurried into the deserted hotel lounge that smelled strongly of beer after the lunch-time trade, there was no sign of him, and her heart sank. The broken bottle of medicine, the lies, the probable parking ticket . . . And all on the basis of a few snatched conversations a year ago and a chance meeting in Oxford—again at tea-time. Why had she been such a fool as to imagine—hope—that Tom might be interested in her? And if he was, how would she respond?

Then suddenly Tom Latimer appeared at the entrance to the bar. He was wearing the green slacks and sweater that were uniform for the staff of Wychwood House, and an old jacket. He didn't look exactly disreputable, but he had clearly made no special effort because he was to meet her. Nevertheless, Alice's spirits soared. And, as she moved across the lounge towards him, it seemed to her that his face lit up with pleasure. It was the most natural thing in the world that he should take both her hands and kiss her.

"Good! You're here," Tom Latimer said. "I was afraid you weren't going to make it."

"I had trouble parking." Alice was breathless.

"You're not as well in with the local police as I am." Latimer grinned at her as he led her to a table in a corner. "We're a bit early," he said, "but they do tea and a nice line in buttered scones here. Just like Oxford. Okay with you?"

"Lovely," she said, delighted that he'd remembered.

He ordered it and after it came they spoke mostly of themselves. If Latimer was reticent Alice scarcely noticed as she did most of the talking. It was rare for her to have an opportunity to discuss her dull, uneventful life, with someone sympathetic—especially when that someone was an attractive male.

"But I must be boring you," she said at last. "Tell me about yourself."

Tom Latimer shook his head. "You don't bore me, Alice, truly you don't. As for me, there's nothing to tell. I've no family, no attachments. Wychwood House is home as far as I'm concerned." It was only half a lie, he thought, and hoped she hadn't heard the bitter undertone in his voice. "To be more exact, I suppose you could say the head gardener's cottage is my home. I room with him and his wife. A bed-sitter. Very convenient. You didn't know?"

"No," Alice said. "That's the little house beyond the hotel's vegetable garden, isn't it?"

"That's right." Tom Latimer hesitated, then he grinned. "I'll show it to you, if you like and you can get away. Thursday. It's my afternoon off." He paused. "We could be alone then," he said. He watched a variety of emotions chase themselves across Alice's face, and felt a rush of affection for her. Impulsively he took her hand in his. "Look, Alice, I don't—"

"Good afternoon to you both!"

Neither of them had paid any attention to the few other people who had come into the lounge in search of tea. Now they stared after the back of a man as he made for the telephone booth, oddly placed at the far end of the lounge. Alice had pulled away her hand as if she had been burnt.

"That—that's Mr. Mortlake," she said. She was already on her feet. "Tom, I must go. I've got Mother's medicine to collect and she'll be worrying—"

"You're afraid he'll tell your parents you were with me—the hotel's odd job man?" Latimer said gently.

Colour flamed in Alice's cheeks. "I don't care a damn what you are!" she said. "But—"

For a moment they looked at each other. Then Latimer said, "I'll hope to see you on Thursday?"

Alice didn't answer. She found her bag and tried to smile. "Thanks for the tea, Tom," she said.

"My pleasure," Tom Latimer said, as he rose to his feet. "My pleasure—Miss Hurley."

# Chapter 4

Before she reserved a room at the Wychwood House Hotel for a three-week stay Cassandra Gray had taken the precaution of making sure that her special requirements could be fulfilled. She was not a demanding guest, she had explained, but certain services were essential to her routine.

First, she needed a large pot of freshly-made coffee at six-thirty each morning. After that she did not want to be disturbed; she would be writing, preferably at a desk or table set in a window with a pleasant view. She would appear at about eleven o'clock, at which time she would like more coffee and a piece of buttered toast served in a lounge. Her room should then be done.

Apart from these quirks, her demands would be no different from those of anyone else. The Kemptons, when they had recovered from their initial surprise at hearing a visitor's requirements spelled out so clearly, had no difficulty in meeting them, and found Miss Gray an ideal guest.

This Wednesday Cassandra Gray's coffee came on time, but its spell failed to work its usual magic. For Miss Gray had been kept awake until the small hours by her neighbours, the Winstons, who appeared to be having a gigantic quarrel, which had gone on and on interminably. She had thought of asking the night porter to intervene, but in the end had decided to bang on the wall—an unlikely necessity in a first-class hotel, she thought.

The result was that she was tired and restless—and, more to the point, was wasting time. She sat at her desk and tried to force herself to work. Her room was at one corner of the house and had windows on two sides. The window before the desk had an especially pleasant view, looking across the lawn and flowerbeds to the path leading to the old stone wall that hid the swimming pool.

As she stared out she saw Vern and Polly Raven jog swiftly by and smiled indulgently, though with a twinge of envy at their youthful enthusiasm—for exercise and, so obviously, for each other. Then Cassandra Gray laughed aloud as they were followed by the stiff-backed figure of Maurice Blair, also in a track suit. The sight of him restored her good humour. He was clearly breathing heavily and in some distress, but he was persevering. She wondered why he made the effort, and vaguely supposed that he might find it irritating that his wife, who took no exercise at all, should continue to look so trim.

She watched him slow as he drew near to the stone wall, thinking at first that he had abandoned his efforts. Then Roy Mortlake appeared in the archway, and it was apparent that Blair had seen him and was prepared to stop and chat.

Mortlake, however, was not prepared to indulge him. With a wave of his hand he moved towards the house, while Blair turned to jog on. It was quite clear, Miss Gray thought, that the early morning walks Mortlake had mentioned after lunch yesterday involved no particular exertion. Unlike the Ravens and Blair, he was not dressed for energetic action but, wearing ordinary slacks and a jacket, he was strolling at a fairly leisurely pace, and as far as Miss Gray could see he showed no sign of heavy breathing.

Invigorated by the small vignette she had just witnessed, Cassandra Gray turned to her work, the alarums of the night forgotten and her exhaustion temporarily overcome.

As the day progressed it grew warm but sultry. Clouds hovered threateningly on the horizon. At lunch everyone seemed to agree that the most must be made of what might well be the last of this unusual spell of summery weather. The swimming pool was popular, for both the active and the passive. The Winstons, their quarrel of last

night apparently forgotten, drove off to Coriston College
to watch their young sons try out for a junior rugger team.
Others—among them the Hurleys—set off to visit nearby
beauty spots or old churches. Some simply went for a
walk. The Fowlers drove into Oxford.

So did Tom Latimer. John Kempton wanted a parcel
collected from the station there, and Paul asked Latimer
to take his sports car, a second-hand Jaguar XK12O in its
original British racing green colour. Paul was proud he
had managed to acquire such a car before it became a
collector's item, but like so many such cars it gave endless
trouble. Today he told Tom that he thought the engine
was running rough, and he'd be glad of Tom's opinion on
it.

Latimer had agreed willingly, glad not to have to take
the hotel's ancient Ford station wagon that he generally
drove on errands. He was an excellent driver, and was
enthusiastic about fast cars. In Oxford, he collected the
parcel, and then took the car on to the dual carriageway
ring road and let it out, keeping an eye open for police
patrols. The speed exhilarated him. He hadn't forgotten
the temptation he'd once had to take a car, any car—steal
one if necessary—do the ton and as a final grand gesture
crash it into a bank or a tree or a bridge support. But he'd
got over that period, and now he could even smile at
himself, if a little sadly.

He eased his foot on the accelerator and listened to
the engine more carefully. He agreed with Paul; after the
high-speed test, it was running rough; he suspected the
fuel supply. Perhaps he'd have a go at it tomorrow afternoon. Then he smiled as he remembered his tentative
date with Alice Hurley, and wondered if she would keep
it. On the whole he guessed she wouldn't, but he hoped
she would and he must be there, just in case. He had no
wish to hurt her. On the contrary, he thought of her with
warmth and affection.

By now he had circled the City of Oxford. He turned
off the ring road and was heading back towards Colombury
and Wychwood House, driving circumspectly in the narrow winding roads. He was nearing the hotel when, around
a bend, he came upon a man walking in the same direc-

tion, but plumb in the middle of what was now little more than a lane. He slowed at once and pressed his finger on the horn. Then the man glanced over his shoulder and Latimer recognized him: it was Mortlake, the unpleasant visitor who had seemed almost to be threatening Mrs. Kempton in the lounge yesterday morning.

Mortlake strode on, ignoring the car, and making no effort to get out of its way, in spite of a further warning hoot. Why the hell should I move over, Mortlake was thinking. Let the damned driver wait! He slowed his pace deliberately.

Tom Latimer's feelings were mixed. Apart from the scene he had witnessed yesterday, he had no particular reason to dislike Mortlake, yet there was something in the man's manner that irritated him. On the other hand, Mortlake was a guest in the hotel, and might well recognize him or the car. Still, there was no reason why he should follow at a walking pace all the way to Wychwood House.

It was a childish ploy, he knew, but very slowly he moved forward, the engine ticking over, until the front of the car was to the left and within a couple of feet of the walking man. Then, prepared to slam on the brakes if Mortlake moved the wrong way, he gave a sudden long blast on the horn.

Mortlake's reaction was all that Latimer could have hoped for. Startled, he jumped sideways to the right and, losing his footing, sprawled in the hedge. Latimer couldn't resist a final derisive hoot as he accelerated past.

Behind him, Roy Mortlake climbed to his feet, shaking his fist after the departing car. In fact, he hadn't recognized Latimer in the brief glance he'd had of the driver, but he had recognized the old green Jaguar. It was a car he had seen parked behind Wychwood House, or one very similar to it.

As soon as he reached the hotel he went round to the garages. Yes, it was the car; if he'd had any doubts a hand on the bonnet told him that the engine was still warm. He stood beside it, breathing hard. A slight misjudgement and that bloody driver might have hurt him badly, even killed him! Or had that been the intention? An apparent hit and run accident?

The thought whipped up his temper which was already close to boiling point. And unfortunately at that moment Paul Kempton came out of the back door of the house and made towards the car. Roy Mortlake watched him.

"This yours?" Mortlake demanded abruptly, kicking the wheel to show his contempt.

"Yes—sir." Mortlake might be a guest at the hotel, but Paul resented his tone. "What of it?"

"You little bastard! Because you own this heap of rubbish you think you own the road, do you?"

"I'm sorry, sir, but I don't know—"

"Or were you having a go at me? I doubt you'd have the guts to kill me, but you could have been trying to scare me off. Was that it? You want me to clear out of your damned hotel?"

"I don't know what you're talking about, sir," Paul said, containing his own temper.

"You don't know what I'm talking about? Don't give me that shit!" Mortlake thrust his face close to Paul's. "I suppose it was your bitch of a mother who put you up to it. Well, sonny, I'll give you a bit of advice—for free. Don't ever try it on again with me, or I'll have your skin for garters—and hers too."

"Now look here—"

"And just so you don't forget what I've said . . ." Savagely and unexpectedly, Mortlake drew back his fist and hit Paul Kempton hard on the side of the chin—harder perhaps than he had intended. The blow sent the young man flying. The back of his head hit the gravel, and for a moment Paul lay still, dazed, as Mortlake strode off.

Before Paul could get to his feet Tom Latimer appeared from the direction of the kitchens. "Paul!" he cried as he ran to help. "Are you all right?"

"I guess I'll live." Paul gently stroked his chin. The skin was only scratched in one place.

"What the hell happened?"

"Mortlake hit me. God knows why! I think he's mad. He more or less accused me of trying to kill him though I can't imagine why—" Paul stopped, remembering Mortlake's interest in the car. "Tom?"

"I know. Yes. I'm sorry. It's my fault." Latimer made the admission at once. "It's me he should have hit, not you, Paul." Briefly he explained what had happened on the road.

"That was damned stupid of you," Paul said. "Whatever possessed you, Tom? After all, he is a visitor at Wychwood House."

"I know. It was silly. I only meant to startle him— teach him not to walk in the middle of these lanes. I didn't expect him to make a major point of it." Latimer shrugged. He wasn't prepared to enter into further explanations, to mention the conversation he'd overheard between Mortlake and Mrs. Kempton, or make more excuses for himself. "If he complains to your father, let me know. Of course I'll carry the can. Or would you rather I told Mr. Kempton myself?"

Paul shook his head. On the face of it, it was a simple matter that had got blown up out of all justifiable proportion. What was more, there was Mortlake's odd reference to Rose. Why on earth should his mother have put him up to kill Roy Mortlake? It made no sense. The man was nuts.

"No," he said. "Forget it, Tom. If it becomes necessary I'll tell Dad, but otherwise it's probably best forgotten."

"Okay," Latimer agreed.

Later that day Paul found himself alone with his father in the office, and decided that it was only fair to retail the story of his encounter with Mortlake. He was astounded at the result. John Kempton was well-known as an easy-going man, tolerant of others' foibles, and very unlikely suddenly to lose control of himself. Now, white around the mouth, he brought his fist down on the desk with a crashing bang. Some papers slid to the floor, but he ignored them. Instead, he cursed Tom Latimer roundly.

Paul stared at him. "Dad, surely it's not that important. I know Mortlake's a visitor and all that, but surely he made an awful fuss about very little. He was in no real danger."

"You don't understand—"

"No, I don't."

"If it had been anyone but Roy Mortlake." John began to pace up and down the small room. "Why, why, did Latimer have to play the fool like that—and with that man of all people, for God's sake?"

"Is it something to do with Mum? Mortlake said he supposed she might have put me up to it. I didn't know what he meant."

John Kempton's stride faltered. He stared hard at his son. Paul, he remembered, was no longer a child. He was an adult, a responsible character. Perhaps, with Mortlake around the place, it was best . . .

Reluctantly, but with no real choice, John Kempton made up his mind. He started to speak slowly, and not entirely coherently. "Yes," he said, "it is—something to do with your mother, I mean. Roy Mortlake used to know her once. Years ago, before I met her. She'd had a bad time. She's told me a good deal about it, though I've never pressed her. She had a miserable childhood. You know she was brought up in care, don't you? A whole succession of foster mothers, each completely indifferent to her existence—or so it seemed to her. When she was sixteen she ran away. As far as she could tell, no one tried to find her. No one cared a damn."

Emotion choked John Kempton's voice. He could see from the expression on his son's face that Paul had guessed what was to come next—or thought he had—and was prepared to discount it. Times had changed. Moral values had changed. So, his mother had had a lover, Paul would think. Roy Mortlake? Not a pleasant guy, but what of it?

John continued. "She was sleeping rough—literally rough—in a public park when this—this man found her and took her home with him. At first, Roy—that's what she always called him, just 'Roy'—was kind to her, and she was reasonably happy. He was out most of the day, and she used to cook and wash and keep their flat clean. Then something went wrong. She never knew the details, but she thought he must have got involved in something illegal—criminal, even. Anyway, they did a moonlight flit together—the first of many—and went up north. They were always moving rooms, as if Roy was on the run. Money was scarce. Roy took to beating her up if she wouldn't do what—what he wanted."

John stopped again. It wasn't easy to explain to your son that his mother had been a whore, even though she'd been effectively forced into it against her will. There was nothing for it but a direct approach, he thought. But if Rose ever discovered that he'd told Paul . . .

He said, "Roy drove her on to the game, as they call it. But not just on to the streets. He wasn't an ordinary pimp. Sure, sometimes he wanted her to get money from the men she slept with, but he chose them himself, and carefully, I gather. Perhaps sometimes it was information he was seeking or favours he was repaying—or blackmail, perhaps. God knows! I don't believe Rose knew either."

But Paul had no time for niceties. "And this Roy is Roy Mortlake?" he demanded.

"Yes, Paul."

"God rot his soul! What the hell's he doing here, then? In our hotel? Our home? Why didn't you throw him out the moment he arrived?" Paul was angry now. "For heaven's sake, Dad, think what Mum must be feeling with him around the place."

"I have thought!" John was grim. "But it's not so easy. What happened was a long time ago. Of course neither of us forgot about it, but we stored it away at the back of our minds like any unpleasant memory. Then out of the blue this guy turns up, Rose is clearly upset, and—I hoped she'd say something to me, but she hasn't."

"I don't understand, Dad. Say what?" Paul shook his head in exasperation. To him the issue seemed simple. Get rid of Mortlake as quickly as possible. Then he paused. "Do you mean you and Mum haven't talked about him since he arrived?" he said in astonishment.

"That's right. Look, never in all these years has she mentioned the man's last name to me, and I've never told her I knew it was Mortlake." John Kempton sighed. "I only found out by chance, and it's much too late now to tell her that I know. Don't you see, Paul, she doesn't *want* me to know. It brings up the past again and makes it much more real and much more hurtful. She wants to *save* me. I suppose she's hoping he'll just go away and she can forget again."

"And will he?"

"I don't know. I doubt it, especially after Latimer's stupidity."

"What happened in the end—before, I mean? Did she leave him?"

"No. He walked out on her, apparently. Left her high and dry, but this time she was lucky. They were living in a room over a pub, and the landlord and his wife took pity on her and gave her a job. Later she moved to London—by herself. She was serving in a bar in Shepherd's Bush when I met her—a very respectable girl. It was only when I wanted to marry her she told me about all this. I wished to God it had never happened, but it made no difference to my feelings. Why should it? She's a wonderful woman, and she's been a wonderful wife to me."

"And the best of mums." Paul was thoughtful. "Okay. I can understand she doesn't want to rake up the past, but if it has to happen, so be it. She'll soon find out it makes no more difference to us now than it has before. We both love her too much for that. As for Mortlake, Dad, I suggest you tell him there was a mistake over his late booking and his room's needed for another guest. Give him a day or two to make other arrangements—but no more. He'll know it's not true, but that doesn't matter. If he becomes unpleasant tell him to go to hell."

"He could become very unpleasant. He could start rumours among the staff and the visitors. That would destroy Rose, and I'd never let anything like that happen, Paul."

Paul Kempton looked his father in the eye. "Nor would I, Dad," he said softly.

# Chapter 5

"Father that was very pleasant, but it wasn't exactly a brisk walk. I need more exercise. I'm putting on weight."

"Nonsense, my dear."

Canon Hurley continued up the drive to Wychwood House with his usual leisurely strides. Beside him, Alice contained her frustration and her irritation, knowing that he wouldn't notice if she suddenly gained ten pounds. She stopped.

"Father, I'm going to leave you here and cut across towards the woods. I really must make the most of this lovely country while I can."

The Canon was forced to stop a few paces ahead of her. "Very well," he said, "but don't go too far, Alice. I don't like the look of those clouds. That storm's been threatening for the last day or two. I shouldn't be at all surprised if it broke before the afternoon's out."

Alice glanced up at the sky. The clouds were lowering, with a coppery sheen that seemed to justify the Canon's warning. If she had intended to go a long way, she might have hesitated. As it was, she could think of no logical reply, so she merely gave a hurried wave and set off across the grass in the direction of the woods.

When she was out of sight she changed course. She also eased her pace so that, strolling along, she appeared to come on the head gardener's cottage by chance. Tom Latimer was sitting on the front step, the door open behind him. He was absorbed in a book and only looked up when Alice had almost reached him.

"Hello!" He sprang to his feet, smiling a welcome. "I'd nearly given up hope of you."

"I'm sorry. I couldn't get here before."

"But you're here now. That's all that matters. Come along in. I'll show you my domain."

Latimer ushered Alice into the cottage. There was a narrow hall from which precipitous stairs led upwards, and doors on the left and right. She expected him to open one of these, but he gestured towards the staircase.

"Upstairs?" she said doubtfully.

"Well, that's where I live," Latimer replied cheerfully. "The family have the ground floor, though I share the bathroom—it's down here too. Believe it or not, we've got every mod. con.—bath, shower, indoor loo—all installed by the kind Kemptons."

"Really?" Alice was unsure how to reply.

She paused on the tiny landing at the top of the stairs, and Latimer reached around her to push open the door ahead. It led into one comparatively large attic room that covered the whole area of the cottage. The room was sparsely furnished, but clean and bright. A couple of colourful rugs covered the varnished floorboards, two armchairs looked well-used and comfortable and the cover on the divan bed matched the curtains. Someone with taste had taken care over the place.

But what immediately struck Alice was the tall bookcase, overflowing with books—mostly paperbacks, to be sure, but books nevertheless. "You read a lot," she said at once.

"It's my main vice."

"Mine too."

Suddenly Alice's doubts left her. She felt relaxed and at home. She went over to the bookcase and started looking at the titles, commenting on those she had read, asking about those she hadn't. If it struck her as unusual that a man employed to do odd jobs at a hotel should like poetry and apparently read Racine in the original, she didn't remark on the fact. And Tom Latimer enjoyed talking books as well as reading them.

It was some while before he said, "Do you know, you've not kissed me yet today, Alice?"

He took her by the shoulders and turned her to him, holding her loosely. It was left to Alice to put her arms around his neck and draw herself close, opening her mouth to receive his tongue. He kissed her lingeringly but gently, then pushed her from him.

"Would you like to make love?" he asked simply.

Somehow Alice was not embarrassed, in spite of the bluntness of the question. "Yes," she said, "but—but don't expect me to be any good at it. I never have before."

The reply didn't altogether surprise Tom Latimer. He laughed aloud. "My dear Alice!" he said. "I'll teach you. Let's start the first lesson now."

Cassandra Gray had walked further than she intended. Because of the threatening weather she had decided to try a wide circle around the hotel, so that she could run for cover if necessary. But in practice this hadn't proved so easy. Lanes and paths didn't always lead in the right directions, and a great deal of zig-zagging was required. Now she felt somewhat tired, so she decided to take a short rest and then make her way straight back to Wychwood House.

She was on high ground and, sitting comfortably on the grass, looked about her. The view across the rolling Cotswold hills was magnificent. She spent several minutes enjoying it.

The sky, however, was darkening and reluctantly Miss Gray was thinking she must leave when she saw a man emerge from some woods below her. Idly, she took her field glasses from their case and focused on him. Immediately she recognized the large figure and thick brown hair of the new guest, Roy Mortlake—out for a walk too, she assumed, losing interest.

A spot of rain fell on her hand and, hastily stowing away her field glasses, she got up from the grass. She hoped she'd be able to reach the hotel before the storm broke and it began to rain in earnest. Her hope, however, was unfulfilled. By the time she reached the grounds of Wychwood House the rain was teeming down and she thought she heard a rumble of thunder.

At the age of sixty Cassandra Gray didn't make a

practice of running, but now she did her best. She arrived, gasping for breath, at the only available nearby shelter—the head gardener's cottage. She huddled inside the porch as she rang the bell, but it was small and offered little protection. If no one were at home she was going to get very wet indeed. She reproached herself for not having brought even a thin raincoat with her. But too late now. She kept her thumb on the bell.

She had almost abandoned hope when at last the door opened. Tom Latimer stood there, wearing the uniform green slacks and a shirt unbuttoned to the waist. His hair was ruffled and he looked as if he might just have woken from sleep.

"I'm sorry to disturb you," Cassandra Gray said, "but I've got caught in the storm. I wonder if . . . " As Latimer continued to block her way, she added sharply, "I'm Miss Gray. I'm staying at the hotel."

"Yes, of course, Miss Gray." Tom Latimer had no option. He took a step back. "Please come in."

"Thank you."

As Miss Gray moved into the hall, there was the sound of a lavatory flushing, then water running. Moments later Alice Hurley emerged from a door at the rear. She was neatly dressed, her hair was tidy and she carried a shoulder-bag. At the sight of Miss Gray she stopped abruptly. Bathing and getting ready to leave as soon as the worst of the storm was over, she hadn't heard the doorbell.

Tom Latimer acted quickly. Turning his back on Miss Gray and blocking her view of Alice, he said, "Miss Hurley, here's another refugee from the storm. If you're all right now, perhaps Miss Gray would like to dry herself in the bathroom. I'll get clean towels."

Given a minute to regain her composure and absorb the clear message that Tom was sending her, Alice responded fairly well. If she seemed flustered at meeting Miss Gray in such unusual circumstances, that was in character. Miss Gray might have accepted the situation at its face value, except for Tom's appearance, the unaccustomed brightness in Alice's eyes, the fact that Alice's clothes were completely dry and the evidence, from the steam in the bathroom, that someone had just had a shower. All in all, Miss Gray was in no doubt about what she had interrupted.

But it was none of her business; in fact, if she'd been asked, she would probably have admitted that she was glad not to have disturbed the two of them sooner. She took longer than she needed to do what she could to dry herself and make herself tidy, allowing them time to speak privately, and she gave the bathroom door a crisp warning bang as she left it.

She found Alice alone. The door of the living-room was open now, and she could see the girl standing by the window, staring out at the rain. "Is it still pouring?" she asked unnecessarily; the drumming of the storm against the cottage was answer enough. "No sign of it clearing?"

"None," Alice said. "But Mr. Latimer is making us some tea, and while we're having it he'll go over to the hotel and bring a car around by road."

"That's very kind of him," Miss Gray said. "We're lucky. Let's hope the other guests who were out walking like us have been as fortunate."

There had been the faintest emphasis on the words "like us," and Alice smiled her thanks with a new assurance. She appreciated that Cassandra Gray had made her point with the utmost tact. And indeed, when they finally reached the hotel, they found that several guests had been caught in the storm. The fact that Miss Gray and Miss Hurley had found convenient shelter in the head gardener's cottage aroused no more than passing interest.

After dinner—excellent, as always—the main topic of conversation among those of the guests who were in the lounge that evening, as the rain beat against the windows and thunder rumbled overhead, was the break in the weather and the chance that it meant the end of the unseasonably sunny and warm spell they had all been enjoying. The consensus was that it looked as if the last of the summer had suddenly disappeared.

Not all the guests were present. Some had already gone to their rooms, including Cassandra Gray, the young Ravens and, pleading a bad headache but in reality yearning to be alone to remember her afternoon, Alice Hurley.

Almost all those who remained were gathered around the
log fire that John Kempton had lit earlier and which was
now blazing merrily. Coffee and liqueurs had been served.
The atmosphere was genial, only slightly disturbed by Mrs.
Hurley's hacking cough, which showed no sign of improve-
ment.

"You really must do something about it, my dear,"
said Mrs. Blair who was a kind soul as long as her kindness
made no demands on her personal comfort. "It sounds
most distressing."

"I'm sorry," Mrs. Hurley apologized, "but it's just the
remains of a bug I've had. I'm assured it's not catching.
Unfortunately the medicine I've been taking doesn't seem
to work."

"I always think lozenges are best for a throat," Mrs.
Fowler volunteered. "William has some wonderful ones.
He gets laryngitis from time to time." She turned to her
husband. "I suppose you didn't bring any with you, did
you, darling?"

"Any what, Anne?" asked William Fowler, who had
been discussing fly fishing with Maurice Blair and the
Canon. "Yes," he said readily enough when she repeated
her question. "I've some in our room. I'll go and get
them. They may help you, Mrs. Hurley. I find them
excellent."

In spite of Margaret Hurley's protests, Fowler insisted
on going to fetch the lozenges immediately. Pausing to
stub out the butt of his cigar as he left the lounge, he
found himself near the corner which the Winstons had
appropriated and forced to catch the tail-end of what had
clearly been a quiet but tense argument between the two
of them. Lady Georgina was seemingly white with emotion
and the Major wasn't mincing his words.

Fowler heard him say, "Pathetic! That's what you are,
Georgie! And that Mortlake man—he's the end, the abso-
lute end!"

Giving his cigar a final stub, William Fowler hurried
from the lounge, afraid that the Winstons might notice his
pause near them and think he was eavesdropping intentionally on what was obviously a private conversation.

He went up to his room, found the lozenges, and was

about to step out into the corridor when he heard Mortlake's voice through the open door of the room next but one. Oh dear, thought Fowler, not again, not another conversation I'm not meant to hear. But the voice sounded particularly harsh and unpleasant, and this time, Fowler stilled his conscience and listened unashamedly.

The point Mortlake seemed to be making was that he had no intention of leaving the hotel. He'd stay as long as he liked and that might be a fair time. If the place was overbooked it was the Kemptons' funeral. The reply was inaudible, but Fowler heard Mortlake say something about having phoned a friend while he was in Colombury last Tuesday to get him to make some inquiries. The voice dropped, but Fowler caught the words, "so I know a lot about little rosebud—more than you do, I guess."

"Little rosebud," thought Fowler. What on earth did that mean? A reference to *Citizen Kane*, of all unlikely topics? Then he became suddenly conscious of his position, and ashamed of listening to yet another private row. He was easing his door shut when he heard John Kempton's voice exclaim, "If you do anything to hurt her, I'll kill you!" Then there was a laugh—presumably Mortlake—a door slammed and steps pounded hurriedly down the corridor.

Minutes later William Fowler returned to the lounge. The Winstons were no longer there. Mrs. Hurley was having another coughing bout and he produced the lozenges. He said nothing to his wife about the two snatches of conversation he had overheard until they were alone and going to bed.

# Chapter 6

By the next morning the storm had cleared, though the ground was very wet, the trees dripped and the flowers and shrubs were heavy with moisture. But the air was fresh, and a pale sun was reflected by the glistening lawns. Vern Raven was eager for his pre-breakfast jog, and pulled a reluctant Polly from their bed.

"It'll be good for you," he said. "Come on, sweetie. Don't be lazy. We'll enjoy it."

Vern was right. After five minutes gentle jogging—hand in hand as always—and breathing great gulps of crisp air, they *were* enjoying it. They made a circuit of the house, and took a path that would eventually lead them across open ground, then via the shrubbery to the swimming pool and on to the front door.

On their way back Polly suggested that they avoid the shrubbery. "The bushes'll be soaking, and it'll all brush off on us."

"Not if we go Indian file and keep to the middle of the path. I know it's narrow, but it's paved underfoot and it'll be a good sight drier than the grass." Vern was determined. "I'll lead the way."

With a shrug of her slim shoulders Polly followed her husband and, as they reached the end of the path and were about to emerge by the pool, she was ready to admit that he'd been right. Then suddenly he stopped dead in front of her. Taken by surprise, she ran into his back.

"Vern! What the—"

"There's someone in the pool."

"So what—" was Polly's first reaction, till Vern moved aside so that she could see where he was pointing.

She drew in her breath sharply. A body lay on its back, arms and legs spreadeagled, on the mosaic floor at the deep end of the pool. Grey flannels, blue blazer, a big man with thick brown hair and a heavy moustache; there was no difficulty in recognizing Roy Mortlake. Vern Raven's hesitation was minimal.

"Quick, Polly. Get help. I'll go in. I guess there's not much chance, but we must try."

Polly Raven ran. Vern had already kicked off his sneakers and dived into the pool. He gasped at the temperature of the water, chilled by yesterday's rain and not heated since, but he was young and strong. Nevertheless, Mortlake, his clothes sodden with water, was no light weight. On his first dive Vern failed to lift him more than a foot or two. It was enough, however, to show that the back of Mortlake's head had been badly damaged. As Vern had suspected, he was unlikely to be alive.

Nevertheless, Vern persevered; he had not spent his childhood vacations at summer camps in upstate New York without learning something. He rose to the surface, took two or three deep breaths to hyperventilate his lungs and dived again. This time he managed to get dual grips under Mortlake's arms and, kicking hard, brought him up and swam the few yards to the side of the pool. But he found it impossible to lift the dead weight out of the water, and had to content himself with keeping Mortlake's head in the air and doing his best to attempt mouth-to-mouth resuscitation. It was no easy matter, and almost certainly quite hopeless.

"Hurry, Polly! Hurry!" he muttered between breaths. The cold was beginning to affect him, and his teeth began to chatter.

Polly was doing her best. Ignoring the path, she had cut across the grass to the house, where Maurice Blair and Alice Hurley were talking together by the front door. They turned as they heard her running footsteps.

"Accident!" she gasped. "In the pool. Man drowned. Go and help Vern! Please!"

She had addressed herself to Blair, from whom she

expected immediate action, but Blair reacted slowly and began to ask questions, while Alice moved quickly. Polly hurried into the house, muttering to herself, "Doctor. Ambulance. Blanket to keep him warm. Police." The last word had come unbidden to her mind and hastily she rejected it. This had been an accident.

Blair quickly recovered from his initial hesitation and followed Alice. Like the Ravens he was wearing a track suit and sneakers; he had just been explaining to Alice the route he intended for his early-morning jog. He soon overtook her, and to Vern's relief, kneeling beside the pool, was able to take some of Mortlake's weight. When Alice arrived, between them they were able to lift Roy Mortlake. As the body came out of the water, Vern, who all this time had been struggling to continue his efforts at the kiss of life paused and glanced at Blair. "We'd better keep it going," he said. "You know what to do?"

Blair swallowed hard. The idea of putting his lips near that sodden face revolted him, but Alice came to his rescue. With surprising efficiency she had been examining Mortlake. "There's no point," she said. "Look at his head." As they stared at the crushed skull, she became aware of the watery grey substance on her hands. Realizing, she ran to the edge of the shrubbery and vomited drily.

Vern Raven sympathized. He felt ill himself and he was grateful for Maurice Blair who, though pale and grim-faced, seemed to have his emotions well under control.

"She's right," Blair said. "Anyone can tell there's nothing to be done for him. He's dead. This is one time the kiss of life won't help." He forced a smile. "All the same, you were splendid trying to save him like that, Mr. Raven."

The younger man made a deprecatory noise. "Vern," he said. "Call me Vern." He was trying to wring water from his track suit. "How do you think it happened?"

Blair shrugged. "Stumbled, I suppose, and hit his head as he fell into the pool, poor chap. Wouldn't you agree, Vern?"

"Yes. Coming out of the shrubbery, perhaps. There are plenty of slippery leaves on the edge thereabouts."

By now further help was assembling. William Fowler

appeared, followed a couple of minutes later by Paul Kempton and Tom Latimer. They stood and looked down at Mortlake's body.

"Dear God!" Paul said. "How—how did it happen?"

"Mr. Raven thinks he slipped on some leaves, hit his head and fell into the pool," Blair said.

"I got him out as soon as I could, but I guess he was dead when Polly and I first saw him. He was face up at the bottom of the pool." Vern Raven was shivering.

Fowler had assessed the situation and took charge. He knelt by Mortlake and inspected the back of his head without touching it. The sight, unpleasant as it was, didn't appear to affect him. He got slowly to his feet.

"Miss Hurley, are you all right?" he said.

Alice, very pale, was standing in the crook of Tom Latimer's arm, leaning against him as if for support. Now she straightened up and Latimer let his arm drop. "Yes," she said. "I'm all right, now—now I've washed my hands in the pool. I'm sorry to have been so stupid."

"My dear, no need to apologize. This must have been a shock for you. It's a shock for everyone. You go along with Mr. Blair and Mr. Raven." He smiled at her encouragingly, then added, "You touched the body, Miss Hurley?"

"Just his head—to—to make sure," Alice said, turning away hastily.

Latimer said, "Sir, if we put Mr. Mortlake on to one of the poolside lounges, Paul and I could carry him back to the house."

"That's a good idea," Paul said. He was almost as pale as Alice, but was making a great effort to control his feelings. "He'll be heavy, but with two of us—"

"No!" The word was spoken quietly, but there was no doubt it was a command. As the two younger men stared at him, William Fowler said, more mildly, "In cases like this, it's better for the doctor to see the body *in situ*, as it were. It's a pity he had to be moved at all, but that was obviously unavoidable."

"Sir, are you suggesting—" Latimer began.

"I'm not suggesting anything," Fowler said affably, "but there'll have to be an inquest, you know. Any unnatural death necessitates an inquest."

"Unnatural?" Paul's voice shook.

"In the sense of sudden or unexpected, when the deceased hasn't been under medical supervision," Fowler explained. "Ah, here's Mr. Kempton, with some blankets. Good. No harm in covering the body decently. Mr. Raven looks as if he needs one, too."

As Fowler went to meet John Kempton, Latimer moved close to Paul. "A pedantic chap, isn't he?" he said of Fowler. "I think what he's really trying to tell us is that he thinks there's a chance Mortlake was murdered."

Detective-Superintendent Thorne was essentially an urban type. He had been born in London, and had spent most of his police career in the "Met." It was only the chance of promotion, combined with Miranda's urgings, that had persuaded him to leave city life and join the Thames Valley Police a few years ago. At first he had been a desk-bound officer at the headquarters of the Force in Kidlington outside Oxford, but he had then transferred to the Serious Crime Squad covering the northern part of the Thames Valley Police area.

He had reluctantly come to admit that life outside the great cities had its advantages—no commuting hassles, less bureaucracy, and, on the whole, a more relaxed environment. He still professed to believe that much of the countryside could benefit from a good dose of asphalt, starting, as he was fond of saying, with his own back lawn.

At the present moment he was sitting in his office regarding his sergeant glumly and stroking his moustache. "Man found dead in swimming pool," he was saying. "Skull bashed in. Body moved at least once. Surrounding area doubtless trampled all over. No obvious motive, I expect. Nothing simple. Guess where!"

"Somewhere on our patch, sir?"

"*Your* patch, Sergeant Abbot. *Your* patch. In other words, not so very far from Colombury. To be precise, the Wychwood House Hotel, where my wife and I were regaling ourselves only a few days ago."

"What?" Abbot, who had been born and bred in Colombury, was shocked. "Who, sir? Not—not one of the Kemptons?"

"You know them?" asked Thorne sharply.

"Not well, sir. But I know of them, and I've met their son, Paul, a few times."

"I see," said the Superintendent. "Well, it wasn't a Kempton. It was a guest in the hotel. A Mr. Roy Mortlake. And, according to Sergeant Court"—Court was the Sergeant in charge of the Colombury Police Station—"Mortlake only checked into the place last Saturday, so he must have made an enemy pretty quickly, unless of course it's his past catching up with him, which will complicate matters further." Thorne sighed.

By now Sergeant Abbot had collected his wits. "Enemy, sir? How do we know it wasn't an accident? People do dive into swimming—"

"Sergeant Abbot, you haven't been paying attention. I said, 'Skull bashed in,' and I'm quoting Dr. Band. He should know, considering he's the local police surgeon, and he says it's hard to see it as accidental. Anyway, Sergeant, the scene of crime boys are already on their way and the pathologist will be too, as soon as they can find the wretched man. Why is it that—? Oh, what the hell! I'm about to phone Mrs. Thorne, and I suggest you call whichever girlfriend you had your eye on for the weekend and warn her you'll be working. Then we'll be off to Wychwood House."

"Yes, sir," Abbot said smartly, silently cursing the loss of his free days.

Three-quarters of an hour later Thorne and Abbot reached Wychwood House, to be greeted by a uniformed constable and John Kempton on the gravel outside the main door of the hotel.

"George—" Kempton began.

"I know, I know," said Thorne, "I'm sorry about all this, but we'll have to talk later."

Kempton nodded miserably, as the constable led the two officers from the Serious Crime Squad to the swimming pool. The Scene of Crime Team was already at work, and the photographers drew back to let Thorne and Abbot view the body. When he'd done this, the Superintendent turned to hs old friend and colleague, Dr. Dick Band, and to Sergeant Court, both of whom he had found waiting for him, together with the Inspector in charge of the Scene of Crime Team.

"Tell me," he said briefly.

Court spoke first. A slow-moving man, in charge of the Colombury Station and in Thorne's opinion, not the most intelligent of officers. But he had a great virtue. He observed Rule One: when in doubt, appeal to headquarters at once; don't let vital evidence get lost or destroyed by waiting hours or even days. Now he explained how he had been called by Dr. Band, and after hearing what the doctor had to say and speaking briefly to some of the inhabitants of the hotel, he had followed this rule.

Thorne turned to Band. "The popular theory," said the doctor, "seems to be that he came out of the shrubbery on one of his regular early-morning walks, went too near the edge of the pool, slipped on some wet leaves, hit his head and drowned."

"And in fact?"

"Well, in the first place, I doubt if it was drowning that killed him, Superintendent. The wound's quite severe enough to have done that by itself. Then, more important, it's hard to match the shape of the wound with the side of the pool. The edge, just conceivably, but I've had a quick look with Sergeant Court, and we can't see any obvious traces of blood or brain matter there, though there's too much water about to be sure. Still, if I had to make a guess, I'd say it was the good old blunt instrument, and wielded with considerable force."

"The area's been cordoned off and we're searching now, sir," said the Inspector. "If the killer—assuming there was one—didn't take the weapon with him, the shrubbery seems a likely place; we're starting there."

"Good," Thorne said absently, moving towards the end of the pool near the shrubbery. "Where exactly was the body when the American chap found it?" he asked Court. "Raven, did you say his name was?"

"That's right, sir," said Court. "According to Mr. Raven it was here, lying flat on its back on the bottom of the pool." He indicated an area in the middle of the pool about nine feet from the end of the pool near to the shrubbery.

"I've got Mr. Raven standing by if you want to see him immediately."

Thorne thought for a moment. "No, leave it." He turned to the Scene of Crime Inspector. "How long will it take to get the pool emptied, do you think? Twenty-four hours?"

"At least that, sir. It's a big volume of water."

"Get it done as soon as possible. In the meantime, make sure you get close-ups and do blood and tissue tests all along the edge of the pool here, and on the whole of this pool wall when you can reach it. Never mind the fact that it's been under water. Go over the rest of the pool when it's dry; I'll get Raven to show how the body was lying."

The Superintendent moved back to Dr. Band, who forestalled him. "I know what you're going to ask, George. Time of death? How long had he been in the water? I can't tell you. I'll have to leave it to the pathologist and the PM. But if you want a blind guess, I'd say not very long in the water—probably not more than an hour. As for how long before that he was hit—if that's what happened—I wouldn't even guess. I take it he was alive last night?"

"I assume so," said Thorne. "We'll have to see. Now, has anyone gone through his pockets? The body's been moved so much there's no reason not to search it."

"Everything's over here, sir," said the Inspector, turning to one of the poolside lounges. And spread out on the vinyl covering were a handkerchief, a bunch of keys and a wallet fat with money.

"That's all?" Thorne said accusingly.

"He was presumably just out for an early-morning walk, sir," said the Inspector. "Anything else'll be in his room. We've sealed it till you had a look, and then we'll go over it with a fine tooth comb."

"Good," said Thorne. "Sergeant Abbot!"

"Yes, sir!"

"Get hold of John Kempton and tell him we'll need a room for interviews. Make sure everything's laid on. Direct external phone line as soon as possible. And other amenities. You know. I'm certain Kempton doesn't want an incident van parked in his front yard."

"I understand, sir." Abbot nodded. George Thorne might have his little quirks, he thought, but on the whole he was a good man to work for. In "other amenities" he included a constant supply of coffee and biscuits, as well as meals when necessary; he liked his food at regular intervals. And at least, Abbot concluded, they should do well in a luxury hotel.

"Then I'll want a complete list of staff and guests, everyone who had a right to be on the premises this morning," Thorne continued. "No one's to leave, of course, until they've been interviewed. If anyone screams, refer him to me. They've all had so much time to talk already, there's no point in trying to keep them apart from each other. After we've had a look at Mortlake's room, we'll get going on the preliminary chats. We'll start with the Ravens."

"Yes, sir," said Abbot, making notes.

"And after them, John Kempton. That should keep us busy till lunch-time. Then the other people who answered the Ravens' appeal for help. The rest will have to wait till last."

One of the detective-constables from the Scene of Crime Team came up to the little group and spoke to his Inspector. "Yes?" said Thorne quickly. "What is it?"

"They may have found the murder weapon, sir," said the Inspector, "and possibly the place where the deceased was killed."

"Show me." Thorne looked at the constable's trousers. "It's wet in there?"

"The shrubs themselves are wet, yes, sir. From yesterday's rain. But the ground around and underneath them is dry enough." The constable glanced sideways at the Superintendent. "Would you like a raincoat, sir?"

"No, thanks." Thorne was wearing one of his better suits today and the thought of what Miranda would say if he returned home with dirty trouser-legs flashed through his mind and made him more abrupt than he intended. "Well, come on then, man. Where is it?"

"This way, sir." The constable wanted to add, "Be careful where you walk," but didn't dare.

He needn't have worried. Superintendent George Thorne was never other than careful at such times. He had known too many occasions when vital evidence had been destroyed as a result of a moment's negligence or inattention. Watching his feet, he followed the constable and his Inspector along the paved path.

Almost at once they came upon another man—a detective-sergeant. He was squatting close beside the narrow path that ran through the shrubbery, and peering at a hydrangea bush through a magnifying-glass, like some latter-day Sherlock Holmes. He was totally absorbed in his task, and ignored Thorne until the Superintendent cleared his throat loudly.

"Oh, it's you, sir," said the sergeant, glancing up. "D'you see where the bush is broken here? There's blood and particles of tissue, if I'm not mistaken. Small bits of bone, too. Some of the victim's skull, sir?"

He stepped back on to the path and handed Thorne the glass, allowing the Superintendent to take his place. Thorne saw at once that the sergeant was probably right. This could well be the place where Roy Mortlake's head was stove in, though at first it was hard to visualize how it could have been done.

Mortlake was a big man. He had clearly been hit from behind, but this particular bush was near the path, and neither the leaves above those bearing the traces nor the other shrubs beside it were damaged. Surely they would have been if Mortlake's whole weight had fallen forward. There was, Thorne finally decided, only one answer.

Mortlake had been squatting down, or had been persuaded to squat down, perhaps to inspect something beneath the hydrangea. This meant that his forward fall would be curtailed. It also meant that his assailant had no need to be tall or very strong; a woman couldn't be excluded. The chances seemed to be that the killer was known to Mortlake, but the attack must have been unexpected.

"Good," said Thorne again. "We'll need photos and samples, of course. Try the other side of the path, too. Maybe our chap stood there waiting for his victim."

"I've looked, sir. Nothing. But I'll go over the area again."

Thorne nodded. If the killer had waited on the path,

rather than in the bushes, it was additional evidence that
Mortlake had known him. But what of the weapon? This
turned out to be a large bottle full of a yellow liquid that
its label suggested was lime juice concentrate. On its base,
blood and matter were visible to the naked eye.

"Dabs?" Thorne queried.

"Don't know yet, sir."

"Let me know at once."

"Sir."

Thorne retraced his steps to the pool. He was well
satisfied with the progress that had been made so far. He
could already to some extent re-create the murderer's ac-
tions. The only puzzling feature was why the murder
weapon had been thrown away so close to the scene of the
attack. Panic? Or disregard of its importance? But, in that
case, why take the trouble to fake an accidental drowning?
Inconsistent? But then murderers—like other criminals—
often were.

A good motive would help, Thorne thought, as he set
off for the house.

# Chapter 7

The room Mortlake had occupied was large and tastefully furnished and decorated, with a deep carpet, wall-to-wall clothes cupboards and two three-quarter-size beds, as well as two dressing-tables, a large television set and a couple of comfortable chairs. Once the seal had been broken, Thorne stood in the doorway, with Abbot, the Inspector and three of his constables behind him. "Whew!" he said. "I wouldn't mind a few weeks here myself."

Apart from its luxurious features the room looked perfectly normal. One bed was rumpled, and a pair of pyjamas and a dressing-gown were draped over one of the chairs. A couple of expensive suitcases stood in a corner. A few newspapers and magazines were piled on a bedside table. The *en suite* bathroom contained a selection of high-class men's toiletries. Thorne opened one of the clothes cupboards, to find a collection of suits and shirts on hangers, socks and underclothes in the fitted drawer unit, and a briefcase at the back, half hidden by a raincoat. The Superintendent pounced, but the case was locked. "I'll take this," he said to the Inspector. "Get your men to work and I'll see you later in the interview room. In the meantime, someone go and bring me the keys from the deceased's pockets."

"Yes, sir," said the Inspector.

John Kempton had allocated to the police as an office and interview room a lounge that had once been the library of Wychwood House. It was now used as an extra area for those who wished to read or write letters, or sometimes have a private snooze. When new guests were shown around the hotel they were tactfully told that it was a "quiet room" where noisy conversations were a little out of place. With some rearrangement of the furniture it made a very suitable and convenient local headquarters for Superintendent Thorne and his colleagues.

Thorne nodded his approval before sitting down behind a writing desk that had been placed so that his back was to a window, and the outdoor light would shine fully on the face of whoever sat opposite him. A phone—not yet a private line, but a direct dial hotel phone—stood beside him on the desk, together with paper for his notes, a carafe of water and a heavy glass ashtray. Moreover, a maid had just brought in a pot of freshly-made coffee and a plate of biscuits. He put Mortlake's briefcase down beside the tray.

Abbot knew his Superintendent. Without being asked he poured the coffee and offered the plate. "Mrs. Dearden will be here in a minute, sir," he said.

"And who's Mrs. Dearden?" Thorne chose two chocolate biscuits.

"The receptionist. She's bringing a list of the guests and the hotel register." Abbot paused. "I got the impression she'd like a word or two with you, sir, and I didn't put her off."

"Oh." In Thorne's experience useful witnesses were rarely eager to come forward.

"This will be her, I expect, sir," Abbot said as there was a tap at the door. He went to open it. "Okay," he said, nodding to the uniformed constable on duty outside, and taking from him Mortlake's bunch of keys. "Come along in, Mrs. Dearden. This is Detective-Superintendent Thorne. Mrs. Dearden, sir."

"Good morning, Mrs. Dearden. Sit down, please. Is it you we should thank for this excellent pot of coffee?"

Thorne indicated the chair across the desk from him and Abbot withdrew to the side of the room, where he could observe and make his notes without being obvious. It was a routine that he and the Superintendent had performed many times, and perfected. They were to repeat it many more times with only slight variations as the owners, staff and guests of the Wychwood House Hotel came under scrutiny.

"I've brought the hotel register and the list you wanted. I've put in the numbers of the rooms the visitors occupied," Helen Dearden said. "It was Mr. Kempton's idea that you might like morning coffee," she added.

"Thank you." Thorne took the leather-bound book and the paper from her, but didn't look at them. Instead, he smiled at her. "Perhaps you'd save me a little time and tell me about Mr. Mortlake yourself, Mrs. Dearden. When he made the booking. How long he was due to stay. That sort of thing."

Helen Dearden sat upright in her chair. She was wearing a navy blue skirt and white blouse. A pleasant, middle-aged woman, she looked efficient and capable. To Thorne, quick to note signs of stress, she looked nervous. He found this mildly interesting; true, many people were apt to be intimidated by police officers, especially senior detectives, but he wouldn't have thought that Mrs. Dearden would be among them.

"Yes, Superintendent. That's precisely what I wanted to tell you because—" She stopped.

"Because, Mrs. Dearden?" Thorne prompted.

"Well, of course I don't know what you're thinking, but—but it must have been an accident. You see, Mr. Mortlake was a completely unexpected visitor. Really he shouldn't have been here at all."

"Indeed? How was that?" Thorne asked.

"He telephoned from London on Saturday morning— out of the blue. He said he wanted to come at once for two or more weeks. Normally that would have been impossible. The hotel's fully booked. But we'd just had a cancellation. One of our regular visitors had to cancel—pressure of work on the Stock Exchange, he said. It was a Mr. Cunningham. He and Mrs. Cunningham come almost every year. It was a double room, of course, but Mr. Mortlake said he didn't mind."

The flow of words was momentarily stemmed, and Thorne said, "He seemed eager to come here?"

"Yes. Very. He said he'd recently had an operation. Nothing serious, but he needed somewhere to recuper-

ate." Helen Dearden hesitated. "He didn't actually say so,
but I got the impression he'd been living abroad and had
no home in England at present. In the register he gave his
address as the London Clinic, Devonshire Place, London,
W.1."

"The London Clinic? Was he a doctor?"

"Oh no. I don't think so. That was where he'd had his
operation. It was his surgeon who suggested Wychwood
House to him, I gather."

"I see," said Thorne thoughtfully. "And that was the
only reason he came here? As far as you know, Mrs.
Dearden, he had no links at all with the hotel? No friends
or acquaintances staying here?"

"No. That's just what I meant. That's why it must
have been an accident." Helen Dearden leant forward as if
to emphasize her words. "Mr. Mortlake was a stranger. No
one here could have any reason to kill him. No one knew
him."

As far as you know, Thorne repeated to himself. She
was being over-emphatic, he thought. A nice woman, but
a poor actress. Was she trying to protect someone? He
changed the subject.

"Have you been the receptionist here for some time,
Mrs. Dearden?"

"Yes. Since my husband died four years ago. But I
knew John and Rose—the Kemptons—before that, when
I worked in London."

"So you're old friends."

"Yes, we are." She sounded positive—almost defiant.

Her manner worried Thorne. He liked the Kemptons,
and hoped they wouldn't prove to be involved. But such
feelings had nothing to do with the case. If anything he
was afraid they tended to make him more rather than less
suspicious of the individuals concerned.

"Let's get back to Mr. Mortlake. What about mail?
Phone calls?"

"No letters or parcels, Superintendent." Helen Dearden relaxed. Clearly she had no objection to this line of
questioning. "As for calls, each room can dial out directly,
but the number of units to be charged are recorded automatically. I'm sure you know the system. Mr. Mortlake

didn't use his phone, except internally to call room service and things like that." Her pleasant face lighted with a sudden smile. "There are no phone charges against him. I checked before I came. I thought you'd want to know."

"Thank you," Thorne said. "And incoming calls?"

"Only one. That was on Wednesday, in the early evening. It was a man's voice. That's all I can tell you."

"You've been very helpful, Mrs. Dearden." Thorne got up, indicating that the interview was over. It was his habit to terminate such interrogations unexpectedly; his experience suggested that if witnesses were left off balance at the end of the first meeting they might well be more forthcoming at the second. It didn't always work, of course, but it was a worthwhile ploy. Neither, unless the witness mentioned the word, did he raise the question of formal statements at what he called his preliminary chats. Abbot could take his notes, but the formalities could be tackled later with those whose evidence showed signs of promise. Again, it was a somewhat unorthodox system, but for Thorne it worked.

As Helen Dearden stood up, he glanced at the list she had given him. "These room numbers—" he said. "A plan of the hotel might be useful. Do you have such a thing?"

"Of course, Superintendent. We have to have plans of each floor to satisfy the fire regulations. I'll send a set along immediately."

"Thank you very much." Thorne nodded at Abbot to open the door and, as Helen Dearden disappeared, said, "Get the clinic story checked, and the cancelled booking."

Almost immediately the Ravens were shown in. They had insisted on being seen together, and Thorne had acquiesced rather than exert his authority at this early stage. Abbot brought another chair forward, and Vern moved it close to Polly before he sat. He had showered and changed into slacks and a cashmere sweater. Polly too had changed, and for once was wearing a skirt in the daytime. Without any effort, or indeed apparent consciousness on their part, they exuded an air of wealth and privilege.

If Thorne had been more aware of the niceties of

American society, he would have muttered something like "Ivy League" to himself. As it was, it was Abbot who was impressed, the more so because the couple were obviously younger than he was. The Superintendent merely smiled at them like a benevolent uncle.

"Now, first of all, Mr. and Mrs. Raven," he said, "tell me in your own words just what happened this morning, as you saw it."

And the Ravens told him, clearly and succinctly. They were inclined to speak in turn and refer to each other for confirmation of detail, but their agreement on the course of events was total. Thorne gave them a high rating as witnesses, and only wished they had had some incentive to be more observant at the time.

"You noticed nothing unusual until you reached the pool?" he asked.

Vern and Polly looked at each other and shook their heads. "No," Vern shrugged. "We were having our morning jog and chatting—mostly about the weather."

"You say you make a habit of a morning jog. Did you usually meet other guests doing the same thing?"

"Sometimes. Mr. Blair jogs," Vern said. "But today he must have started out later than we did, because—"

"Because I found him talking with Miss Hurley by the front door when I came running for help," Polly concluded.

"And Mr. Mortlake—I wouldn't call it jogging, but he used to take an early walk. We've met him once or twice," Vern said.

"But this morning you saw no one?"

"No," Vern said.

"Yes." For the first time Polly contradicted her husband. "I saw Tom Latimer."

"Did you? Where? You never told me." Vern was reproachful. "Latimer's one of the staff. He seems to do anything, anywhere in the hotel," he explained to the Superintendent.

Thorne nodded, concentrated on Polly. He remembered Tom Latimer, the pleasant young man who had parked their car for them on the day he and Miranda lunched at Wychwood House, and who had seemed famil-

iar, though he'd not been able to place him. He repeated
Vern's question, "Where did you see him, Mrs. Raven?"

Surprisingly Polly looked uncomfortable. "He was near
the shrubbery. Not the pool side," she added quickly.
"The other side, where the grounds are more open. I only
caught a glimpse of him in the distance as we were jogging
round. He was sort of half hidden by a tree." She turned
to Vern. "I didn't mention it at the time because you were
talking and it didn't seem to matter."

"It probably doesn't." Thorne sounded reassuring.
"But Mr. Latimer may himself have seen something useful."

"Sure." Polly was obviously relieved. "I didn't want
to be kind of—kind of pointing a finger at him," she said.

Thorne nodded his understanding, smiling benevo-
lently again. He asked a few more questions, elicited a
promise that next day, when the pool had been completely emptied, Vern would demonstrate where and how
Mortlake's body had been lying, and let the Ravens go.

John Kempton was next on the list, and while he was
being summoned, the constable on the door handed a
note to Abbot, who passed on the substance of it to
Thorne. "Mrs. Dearden's information's been checked and
found correct, sir. The Cunninghams did cancel early
Saturday morning. They've never heard of anyone called
Mortlake. But the London Clinic has. He had a hernia
operation there. The surgeon doesn't remember, but he
may well have recommended Wychwood House; he had
an aunt who used to stay here. He visited her occasionally
and liked the place."

"Therefore Mortlake apparently came here unexpectedly and by chance." Thorne grunted, and flipped through
some pages of the hotel register. "He was the last guest to
arrive, apart from Canon Hurley and his family, so no one
followed him here—at least not to stay in the hotel. Either
he had an old enemy in the vicinity, or he made a new
one in the space of a few days."

"It would be quick work, sir," said Abbot.

"Quite," Thorne agreed.

John Kempton's arrival prevented further discussion.
Kempton was far from his normal, cheerful self. Indeed,
he looked more grim and haggard than Thorne had ex-

pected. Abruptly he pulled back the chair in front of the desk so that he wouldn't be directly in the light from the window, and sat.

"This is damned awful, George," he said. "Damned awful! Rose is worried sick. We both are. It's the sort of thing that could ruin the hotel. Is there any chance it could be an accident?"

"Sergeant Court told me you saw the body. What do you think?"

Kempton didn't answer. He nibbled at his bottom lip and shook his head slowly. At last he said, "What happens now? Police all over the place, I suppose. Our visitors being questioned. Then the media'll get on to it. Plenty of ghastly publicity."

Thorne, who knew Kempton as a kindly, good-natured man, noticed that he expressed no regret at Roy Mortlake's death, only at the manner of it. "I know," he said. "The sooner we can clear up the case, the better for you and everyone. But at the moment I'm in the dark. Tell me what you know about Mortlake, John."

Kempton repeated what Helen Dearden had already reported. Then unexpectedly he added, "I know one's not meant to speak ill of the dead, but Mortlake was an—an unpleasant chap. A bullying type. Thought he was little Lord Muck." He paused as if aware of sounding too savage, and continued more mildly. "He had a foul temper. The day before yesterday, for no good reason, he—he knocked down my boy."

"He knocked Paul down? Literally? With his fist?" Thorne frowned in surprise.

"Yes. Right on the chin, without giving him a chance to explain, or anything."

"Explain what?"

Kempton told the story of the Jaguar, and the mistake Mortlake had made. "But even if Paul *had* been driving," he said, "there was no excuse for attacking him like that. Mortlake wasn't hurt; he wasn't ever in any danger, though it was lucky Latimer was going slowly. Mortlake just wouldn't get out of the way. He was just being bloody-minded. He could easily have let the car pass." Kempton shrugged. "At least that's what Tom said when I tackled him after Paul told me about it. I ticked Tom off, I had to. After all, it was a bloody stupid thing to do to a visitor. But I must admit I'd have been tempted myself."

"And that's all you know about Roy Mortlake?"

Kempton half turned in his chair so that he could look Thorne straight in the eye. "That's all I know about him," he said.

"Right," said the Superintendent. What he thought was: when they stare at you like that they're always lying; I wonder what John's trying to hide. But, as usual, he didn't press the point immediately. Instead, he said, "Tell me more about this chap Latimer. How long's he been employed by you?"

"About two years—and he's a splendid worker. He'll do anything, and he gets on with a job whether you're there or not. He's reliable—and he uses his initiative." Kempton gave a short laugh. "To be honest, we've become quite dependent on him."

Thorne's answering smile was thin. "How did you find this—this paragon?"

"I didn't find him. He found me." Kempton was obviously more at ease now that they were no longer discussing Mortlake. "He turned up one day, said he was broke, had been living like a tramp, needed a job, any job—"

"No references?"

"No. Okay, George, I know I was taking a risk, but I've been down on my luck myself in the past, and I liked the man. He's well-spoken, you know, and I suppose I thought he might have had a row with his family or his wife or something. Anyway, he was pretty reticent and I didn't ask too many questions, but I was careful enough to start him off on outside work—that's how he came to be living in the head gardener's place. And it's paid off. I couldn't hope for a better odd job man, for want of a better title. If ever Tom wants to leave here, he can have the best possible references. What more can I say?"

"Not much." Thorne was asking himself the obvious question: could Latimer and Mortlake have had some previous connection?

A rap on the door signalled the presence of the In-

spector in charge of the Scene of Crime Team, and gave
Thorne an excuse to end his interview with Kempton.
He'd study all the reports later on paper, but he wanted
the Inspector to give him the gist of them immediately.
He listened with attention.

The pathologist had been and gone, promising to do
the PM as soon as possible, and the body had been removed. The pathologist's first reaction had been similar to
Dr. Band's, that the head wound by itself had been fatal.
No immediate guess about time of death was possible; the
immersion of the body had complicated that calculation.
The pool was draining. The shrubbery was still being
searched, as well as the rest of the pool area, but nothing
more had been found. There were no fingerprints at all on
the bottle of lime juice.

"Probably wound a handkerchief round it," Thorne
muttered. "Anything else?"

"The deceased's room," reported the Inspector. "Everything he owned is of high quality, and some of the clothes
have Canadian labels. One of the magazines and some of
the things in the bathroom are Canadian."

Thorne stared at Mortlake's briefcase on the desk
beside him. "Let's try this next," he said, producing the
bunch of keys. His first attempt was successful. The most
interesting documents the case contained were two passports, one blue and British, the other green and Canadian, two Canadian cheque-books from a bank in Calgary,
Alberta, a few bank statements and papers concerned with
investments managed by a Trust Company, also in Calgary, an out-of-date yellow book of international certifi-
cates of vaccination and a receipt from the London Clinic.

Thorne examined the passports with interest. They
were clearly both Mortlake's. The British one, now dog-
eared and expired, included a Canadian entry stamp, showing that Mortlake had entered the country as a landed
immigrant nearly twenty years ago. A folded piece of stiff
green paper fell out of the book; it was a Canadian Citi-
zenship Certificate. Mortlake had acquired Canadian citi-
zenship just five and a half years after he had arrived there,
and the Canadian passport proved that he had travelled on
it ever since.

The Superintendent pondered over these documents for a moment, and passed them to Abbot without comment. Next, he picked up the bank and trust company papers. "Phew!" he said for the second time that morning. "Our friend must have struck it rich over there. Not that it's done him much good."

He turned to Abbot. "Okay. You know what the next step is. Get on to the Met and see what they can find out from the RCMP, or the Calgary police, if the place has a force of its own."

# Chapter 8

The preliminary inquiries continued after lunch. Interviews with those who had been next on the scene—those who had responded quickly to Polly Raven's appeal for help—would form the afternoon's work.

"I'm sorry to meet you again in these circumstances," Thorne said when Maurice Blair was shown in.

Blair replied very civilly, told his story simply, and sounded genuinely sorry at Mortlake's death. "Poor devil," he said. "England's not done well by him, has it? First an operation, and now this. He was on holiday from Canada, you know. Went out there years ago—to make his fortune, I suppose. And I gather he succeeded. He hadn't been back in the old country for ages."

"You sound as if you were friendly with him, Mr. Blair," Thorne said. "Did you know him previously?"

Blair shook his head. "No, I'd never seen him before he arrived at Wychwood House, but I probably got to know him better than anyone else here, though that's not saying much. I met him by chance out walking yesterday, and we chatted as we hurried back to the hotel through the storm. Otherwise, we've scarcely done more than pass the time of day. Nevertheless, it's a shock to get a man's brains all over your track suit. I tell you, I shan't be wearing it again."

"When you reached the pool and were helping Mr. Raven pull the body from the water, what did you think, Mr. Blair?"

Blair looked blank. "What do you mean—what did I

think? I didn't think anything, except that he was heavy, and I must try to stop Miss Hurley from seeing the back of his head. I'm not even sure I realized he was dead at that point. Though, thinking back, I should have done."

"Why?"

"Why?" Blair stared at Thorne. "If half your brains are falling out of your head and you've been found at the bottom of the deep end of a swimming pool, there's a fair chance you're dead, wouldn't you say?" He paused. "I could have put that better," he added. "I'm sorry."

Thorne made no direct comment. "When you did realize he was dead," he asked, "how did you imagine it had happened?"

"Young Vern Raven suggested he must have slipped on wet leaves, knocked himself out and slid into the pool. Maybe I was stupid, but there wasn't much time to consider the matter before Mr. Fowler was implying it might not have been an accident. Then I saw the point, though even now I find it hard to believe. What motive could there be? Mortlake can't have had any enemies here, can he? As far as I could see, he hardly knew anyone."

Again the Superintendent didn't comment. He merely thanked Blair for his help and dismissed him politely. Thorne himself found the situation hard to credit. But someone had undeniably disliked Mortlake enough—or feared him enough—to smash his head in with a bottle full of lime juice. As a method of murder it at least showed signs of originality.

Abbot sighed heavily. He should know by now, he thought. This was typical of the Superintendent. Though Blair had been on the scene almost as soon as the body was found, he had contributed nothing. Just when he might have been backed into a corner Thorne had let him go. Abbot could foresee a succession of equally ambiguous interviews. He could only hope that Thorne didn't intend to speak separately to everyone in the hotel, or they'd be here till next week. Then he reminded himself that the Superintendent's methods often paid off. The only thing he really had against his superior was that Thorne didn't take him into his confidence as frequently as he might.

But, he reflected, Thorne often checked up on him to see
how he was following the logic of the proceedings. He
sighed again, and heaved himself to his feet as Alice
Hurley was ushered in.

Alice corroborated what Blair had said. She was chatting to him at the front door of the hotel when Mrs. Raven
had come running. It was clear that she had kept her head
and done what she could to help.

When his turn came William Fowler took the initiative by reminding Thorne of their meeting in happier
circumstances a few days ago. Remembering this witness's
legal background, Thorne took the precaution of explaining that this interview was merely preliminary and that
formal statements might be required at a later stage.

Fowler nodded and told his very similar story; he was
passing through the hall on his way to breakfast in the
dining-room when Mrs. Raven had dashed in the front
door. "As soon as I gathered the gist of what had happened, I decided to set off for the pool," Fowler said.

"Who else was in the hall?" Thorne asked.

"Young Kempton was behind the reception desk,"
Fowler said. "I told him to phone a doctor and I got one of
the maids to take care of Mrs. Raven; I suspected the shock
was beginning to catch up with her." He thought for a
moment. "I can't recall anyone else."

"But I understand that Tom Latimer, the man who
does odd jobs around the place, was—"

"Not then. He turned up at the pool with Paul
Kempton," Fowler corrected the Superintendent.

"Ah!" said Thorne as if this was news to him. "And
Sergeant Court tells me you stopped them from moving
the body more than necessary."

"Yes." Fowler spoke a little pompously, even stiffly.
"As I told you the other day, Superintendent, I spent my
working life as an officer of the Court. I'm not sure whether
I mentioned that the firm of which I was a partner had an
extensive criminal practice, so I'm not unaware of pro-
cedural matters. I didn't know, of course, but I feared that
a crime might have been committed, and I took the steps
that seemed appropriate."

"Sir, we're very grateful for your intervention. It may well have made our task that much simpler," Thorne said smoothly. He couldn't imagine why, but in some way he seemed to have offended William Fowler. He decided to end this first meeting quickly. "And there's nothing else you can tell me, sir? With your experience . . ."

The Superintendent let the phrase hang, and Abbot in the background thought, he's done it again, the old devil. Fowler was immediately mollified.

"Not really, Superintendent." Fowler hesitated, torn between dislike of repeating overheard conversations and his duty to cooperate with the police. He finally decided to compromise. "For such as it's worth," he said, forcing himself to speak lightly, "I got the impression that Mortlake was inclined to put people's backs up a little. I've no idea why; perhaps the matters concerned were perfectly trivial. For instance, by chance I overheard Major Winston saying something about Mortlake being the end—"

"When was this, sir, and what did you understand by it?"

Unknowingly, the Superintendent had made a tactical error. Fowler, who had been about to make a casual reference to the argument between Mortlake and John Kempton that he'd also overheard, was distracted by Thorne's interruption. "Last night after dinner," he said shortly, "and I made nothing of the remark. You'll have to ask Major Winston."

"I'll certainly do that, Mr. Fowler. I'm grateful to you. Thank you, sir."

The Superintendent was on his feet. The telephone was ringing. William Fowler's opportunity casually to mention Kempton's disagreement with Mortlake had passed. With some relief he nodded to Thorne and Abbot, who had answered the phone, and went.

As the door shut behind him, Abbot, still holding the receiver, said, "Mrs. Dearden wants to know if we'll be staying for dinner, sir."

"Of course we'll be here," Thorne said at once. "We won't get a better dinner in Colombury, not if that lunch was anything to go by."

"Sir."

Thorne was ruminating, stroking his moustache. "Sergeant Abbot," he said suddenly, "what did you make of Fowler?"

"He seems to have taken charge, acted responsibly. But he's a lawyer, so you'd expect him to." Abbot frowned, turning the pages of his notebook and trying to recall the nuances of the interview. "He struck me as a bit—odd—about this Major Winston. I—I thought you might have pressed him on that, sir."

Thorne nodded his understanding. "I'd rather let him stew," he said. "We'll get more out of him that way in the end. Anyway, it's early days yet. Let's have young Kempton in, and get Latimer, but keep him outside till I give you the nod. Then bring him in quietly. I've an idea Tom Latimer might be as interesting as any of them."

Paul Kempton arrived promptly. He was wary, almost aggressive. He didn't wait for any questions, but said immediately, "Dad warned me he'd told you about the— the run-in I had with Mr. Mortlake. It was ludicrous. But if you want to know if I bore the guy a grudge, I did. My chin still hurts where he hit me. So I suppose I had a motive, but I didn't kill him."

"No one's suggested you did, Paul," Thorne said mildly. "Now, tell me about this morning. You were in the hall when Mrs. Raven arrived, you called Dr. Band, and set off for the pool—with Tom Latimer. Is that right?"

"More or less. I met Tom as I came out of the house and shouted to him." He looked doubtful. "We weren't the first there," he added firmly. "Mr. Fowler and . . ."

Thorne let him talk, but learnt nothing new. When Paul paused, he said, "I meant to ask your Father, but you'll know just as well. You serve drinks by the pool, don't you, and morning coffee and tea?" He gave Abbot a brief nod and the Sergeant got up and left the room.

Paul Kempton stared. "Yes, anything people want," he said. "Sandwiches or snacks sometimes, if they ask for them. Why?"

Thorne ignored the question. "And do the waiters take the bottles and glasses and things out each day? Or do you keep any stocks outside?"

"No, there's nowhere to put anything."

"That must be inconvenient."

"Not really. We've thought of installing storage cupboards behind the marble bar, but it's never seemed worth it. Superintendent, I don't understand. What's this got to do with Mortlake?"

"Probably nothing, but bear with me a moment, Paul. Tell me how it works, in detail, please. Do you use trays or trolleys or—"

Paul Kempton looked at the Superintendent with a mixture of pity and distrust. "Well, if you really want to know—" he said.

In fact Thorne couldn't have cared less. He was waiting for the opening door to herald the arrival of Abbot with Tom Latimer. When the moment came, he broke in on Paul's account without apology. "What you're saying, then, is that it's not improbable that a barman could overlook an odd bottle out by the pool. Not liquor, perhaps—that would have to be accounted for. More likely a bottle of—lime juice, say, or something like that."

"It's not impossible, no, Superintendent. It's been known to happen. We lose teaspoons out there from time to time too."

Paul's bewilderment had given way to amusement, and he was grinning broadly. The Superintendent scarcely noticed. He was watching the play of emotion across Latimer's face as he stood in the doorway and heard the last few exchanges. His expression quickly settled into a mask of indifference, and Thorne found it difficult to be certain of the result of his experiment, though he felt there was little doubt that Latimer had been startled at the mention of a bottle of lime juice—a potential blunt instrument.

"Right, Paul. Thanks," Thorne said. "I'll talk to Mr. Latimer now."

Paul, who had been unaware of Latimer's appearance, turned in surprise. He gave Latimer an encouraging wink as he relinquished his seat to him, but Latimer didn't respond. Nor did he respond to Thorne's interrogation, answering each question with a monosyllable when possible, or with a terseness that was almost rude. He kept his gaze firmly fixed on the desk separating him from the Superintendent.

"Had you ever met Mr. Mortlake before Monday last?" "No." "Why did you almost run him down with Paul Kempton's car?" "He wouldn't get out of my way." "No other reason?" "No." "You disliked him, didn't you?" "Yes." "Why?" "Why not?"

The Superintendent began to get annoyed. "What were you doing near the shrubbery early this morning?"

"My job."

"What do you mean by that?"

"Looking to see if yesterday's storm had caused any damage." It was the longest answer that Latimer had volunteered.

"Did you go into the shrubbery."

"No."

"Not even though it's on your way to the grounds beyond?"

"No."

Again it was a careless negative. Though Latimer must have realized the implications of this line of questioning he showed no reaction, but continued to stare at the desk without making any effort to meet Thorne's eyes. A more accomplished liar than John Kempton, Thorne thought, if indeed he were lying.

"Did you see anyone else around while you were doing your—your job?"

"Mr. and Mrs. Raven." For once Latimer appeared to give the inquiry some thought. "And old Canon Hurley."

"Miss Hurley's father?" asked Thorne in some surprise. "Was he in the shrubbery?"

Latimer spotted the trap and smiled. He raised his eyes at last. "I wouldn't know," he said deliberately. "I told you. I didn't go into the shrubbery."

"So you did," Thorne admitted. "That'll be all for the moment. Thank you." He stood up and came round the desk. As he did so, his arm brushed across its surface and knocked the glass ashtray to the carpeted floor in front of Latimer. It was an involuntary response for Latimer to pick it up and replace it.

"That one's got something to hide," Thorne said when Abbot had closed the door behind Latimer. "Thomas Latimer? I'd not heard the name before I came to lunch here and my wife mentioned it. Mrs. Kempton had told her who he was. But I know I've seen the face somewhere."

The Superintendent shook his head, and stared at the ashtray. "Treat it carefully, Sergeant Abbot," he concluded. "If we don't find those dabs in records I'll stand you your next half-dozen pints."

# Chapter 9

A large number of the inhabitants—management, staff and guests—of the Wychwood House Hotel found it hard to sleep that Friday night. No one was grieving for Roy Mortlake, but his death affected many of them in one way or another.

John and Rose Kempton had talked in low voices for what seemed like hours, and then Rose had wept till she was exhausted. Now she lay beside her husband, his arm around her, her head in the hollow of his shoulder. Since they had come to their room he had held nothing back from her. She knew how he had come to recognize Roy Mortlake, and how he had watched with anxiety and understanding as she became literally sick with worry. She knew that, after Mortlake's attack on Paul, John had asked the dreadful man to leave the hotel, and she knew that Mortlake had refused.

"I wished him dead. What's the point of pretending otherwise? But I didn't kill him, love." John spoke again. "You do believe me, don't you, Rose?"

"I believe you," Rose said. And she could only pray that what John said was true. Her husband was slow to anger but he could be roused to action; one night years ago she had seen him throw a drunk across the pub because he'd tried to molest a girl. "But if Thorne finds out about me and Roy he'll think you had a motive. You and Paul, both," she added suddenly. "Oh God, John, why did you have to tell Paul?"

"Because Mortlake had already let on there'd been

something between you and him. Paul's not a fool, Rose.
Better for him to learn some of the truth than be bothered
by innuendo. Darling, all he knows is that once—a long
while ago—you lived with Mortlake, and he gave you a
bad time," Kempton lied. "Don't worry about Paul. He
loves you."

"I love him too, you and him. You're all I've got.
John, if anything happened to either of you because of me
I don't know what I'd do."

"Nothing's going to happen." Kempton stroked Rose's
hair. He was determined to reassure her. "Thorne won't
find out you ever knew Mortlake. How could he?"

"There—there *are* records, John."

"So what?"

"John, there's something else—something you don't
know, something I've never told you. I—I was married to
Roy Mortlake once. Legally, in a Registrar's office. He
said it would be more convenient if we were properly
married. Perhaps it made his men friends feel safer with
me. I don't know . . ." She couldn't go on.

Kempton pulled away from her and sat up. He cursed
aloud. "Damn him to hell!" he said. Marriages, births,
deaths were the simplest things in the world to trace and
check, and the Superintendent wouldn't fail to go through
the motions; he'd want to know the total history of the late
Roy Mortlake—it would be part of the routine.

At length he said, "Rose, George Thorne is an
understanding man and a bright one. He's not about to
suspect me or Paul of killing Mortlake because years ago
you were married to him and—and he mistreated you."

"No—no. Not if it was only that, but—"

"You mean Thorne'll think Mortlake could have been
threatening a spot of blackmail. Free board and lodging
for as long as he wants, or he spreads some filthy tales
about you, so visitors'll think twice about coming here?"
John Kempton laughed mirthlessly. "God! That wouldn't
have done half as much harm to the hotel as finding one of
the guests in the swimming pool with no back to his head.
I bet you anything that as soon as Thorne gives permission
the place will empty, and heaven knows when it'll be full

again. No, if I'd been going to kill Mortlake, I'd hardly have done it on the premises. Thorne'll see that."

Rose made no reply, and for a moment or two they were silent. Then Kempton said gently, "Love, I'm not sure it wouldn't be best if we told Thorne ourselves. Just about the marriage. We don't have to mention the—the things Mortlake made you do."

"No, John, we mustn't!" Rose pulled herself away from his encircling arm and sat up. She spoke urgently, "We can't!"

"But why not, love?"

Rose was taking great, heaving breaths. Even now she couldn't bring herself to tell John the whole truth. The rest he had somehow managed to accept, but this—this would be the last straw. Maybe Thorne would just assume . . . She could only hope. Then the thought occurred to her that perhaps the Superintendent already knew, perhaps Mortlake had told someone who had told him.

"Because—because I'm afraid," she said, and she thought with bitterness that indeed she was telling the truth.


William Fowler was also awake. Over the years he had acquired a great deal of respect for John Kempton, his hotel-keeping, his treatment of his guests, his business methods. Now he was wondering why Kempton had probably lied to him and what, if anything, he should do about it.

Ironically enough the chef had surpassed himself that evening, though scarcely anyone had enjoyed his dinner and many had left it half-eaten. After the meal, most of the visitors had shunned the lounges and gone straight to their rooms. Fowler had sought out John Kempton and reluctantly admitted to overhearing part of Kempton's conversation with Mortlake the previous evening.

"None of my business, I appreciate, John, but embarrassing in the circumstances, and I know you'll forgive me for raising the matter. I've not mentioned it to the police because I felt sure there was some reasonable explanation."

What Kempton had said was, in fact, reasonable enough

on the surface. According to him, Mortlake, blaming Paul for Tom Latimer's crass stupidity, had taken a punch at Paul. "After some thought I decided it would be best for everyone if I asked Mr. Mortlake to leave the hotel at his earliest convenience," Kempton had said. "We had a bit of an argument when he refused. That's all. Nothing serious. Naturally I had to acquiesce in Mortlake's decision. Incidentally, Superintendent Thorne already knows all about it."

Even at the time, Fowler thought, he'd been unhappy with Kempton's explanation. His every instinct had warned him—still warned him—not to accept it. It might be the truth, but it wasn't the whole truth and nothing but the truth. As he tried to remember the exact words he'd heard, and the tone in which they'd been spoken, they somehow failed to fit with Kempton's story. Nor did the phrase "a bit of an argument" accord with the impression he'd received of suppressed but furious anger.

Anne, hearing the tale as they were undressing to go to bed, had advised him to forget it. There was nothing he could or should do, she said. She was more concerned with the cancellation or otherwise of their fortieth wedding anniversary party. Personally, he had every wish to abandon the project, but in the end they agreed they wouldn't, if only to help the Kemptons by adding a degree of normalcy to proceedings at Wychwood House.

Sighing, Fowler tried to compose himself for sleep.

Several rooms away Canon Hurley had given up all hope of sleep. Nor could he pray, though now, in the middle of the night, he was kneeling by his bed in an attitude of devotion, familiar words coming to his lips while his thoughts were elsewhere. Like William Fowler, his conscience troubled him. He too had information about Roy Mortlake that the police would be glad to have.

Margaret Hurley coughed in her sleep and, lifting his head from his hands, the Canon gave his wife a bitter glance. If she hadn't woken him with her coughing yesterday morning he'd never have gone for that unaccustomed walk before breakfast. It wasn't a habit of his to rise so early on holidays. Usually, he stayed in bed, awaiting his

early-morning tea. If only he'd followed his routine yesterday, he thought.

Rising stiffly from his knees and shivering slightly,
Canon Hurley found his dressing-gown and sat in an armchair. His legs stretched, his shoulders hunched, he stared
into space. His thoughts were concentrated on his daughter, sleeping fitfully in the adjoining room.

He supposed it was his fault, his and Margaret's.
These days parents were expected to take any blame, and
it was true that by modern standards Alice led a dull life.
But she had always been a quiet girl, seemingly content.
He tried to remember how old she was. He wasn't sure.
Probably it was time she was married, but . . .

Anger welled up in him. That wretched man Mortlake
and his insinuations! More than insinuations. Not only had
he suggested that the Canon was on his way to the head
gardener's cottage in search of his daughter but, when this
remark met with incomprehension, he'd laughed coarsely
and stated bluntly that Alice was having an affair with Tom
Latimer. He'd seen them together in Colombury on Tuesday, holding hands at the Windrush Arms, and one had
only got to look at her to see the girl was asking for it.
How long had they been "having it off"? These were the
words Mortlake had used, though the Canon could hardly
bear to recall them. Anyway, good luck to them, the man
had said. Maybe, if he hurried, the Canon would catch
them at it.

Canon Hurley winced at the memory of the conversation, and the foul language the man had used. He was glad
Mortlake was dead. Glad! Now at least he couldn't spread
his filthy stories about Alice any further. If only he'd
died . . . Suddenly seeing in his mind the body sprawled on
the path and the shattered skull, the Canon shivered again
convulsively.

At the same moment Cassandra Gray had been dream-
ing about Canon Hurley. She woke with a start, and was
relieved immediately to recall an obvious explanation. She
had been thinking of the Canon before she went to sleep,
and wondering if she should tell the police what she had
seen that morning. Her abrupt awakening was equally

easily explained: a sharp noise from the Winstons' room next door.

Cassandra sighed. Another row, she thought, and there's nothing I can do about it. She slid down into the bed, pulled the bedclothes over her head and hoped to hear no more.

In fact, Miss Gray was wrong. The Winstons were not quarrelling, for the simple reason that Major Winston was not present. What Miss Gray had heard was Lady Georgina crying out in a spasm of frustrated misery. Lady Georgina was alone, unhappy and frightened. Derek Winston had apparently disappeared.

Georgina had woken the previous morning to find the bed beside hers empty. This in itself was unusual; Derek never got up before nine if he could possibly avoid it. She had dressed and gone to look for him, but he was nowhere in the hotel. And when she came back from the garage, having discovered that their car was missing, she had learnt that Roy Mortlake was dead.

She had spent most of the day on the telephone. She had tried their London house, their country cottage, the offices that her husband spasmodically attended, his several clubs, then family, friends, even acquaintances. Her excuses for calling became more and more improbable, and her inquiries more and more convoluted. Finally she phoned Coriston College, terrified that Derek might have taken the boys away, but the headmaster assured her in a surprised voice that they were both safely in school.

This, at least, was a relief. She had a light dinner in her room to avoid the other guests and somehow managed to get through the evening. Apparently her husband's absence had gone unnoticed in the general confusion caused by what the maid who brought her meal told her was now a murder investigation. But sleep was an impossibility. Never before, however fierce their quarrel, had Derek walked out on her without some indication of his destination. Admittedly their last row had been different. For once, instead of Derek making a pass at some young girl, it was she who had provoked him by deliberately throwing herself at Roy Mortlake. It had damn well served Derek

right, she thought, angry in her misery, but she hadn't
expected him to take it quite so seriously.

Roy Mortlake murdered, Derek missing. As the night
wore on, without rest, without sleep, her frustration grew.
Finally it burst, and she groaned aloud.


At the other end of the hotel the Blairs, too, were
awake, and as near as they ever got to quarrelling. Maurice Blair's patience with his wife was at a particularly low
ebb. Normally he didn't use sleeping pills, but the horror
of Mortlake's death had affected him and, sure he wouldn't
sleep, he had taken two of his wife's Mogadon capsules.
When she had insisted on awakening him at one in the
morning he had difficulty in containing his temper.

"For heaven's sake, Nina," he said irritably. "It's
been a ghastly day. Do we have to mull it over again in
the middle of the night?"

"I can't sleep for thinking of it, Maurice, wondering
who might be next."

"What?"

"It could be you. After all, you were the first responsible person on the scene. One can't count those young
Americans or Alice Hurley. Maybe you saw something the
murderer didn't want you to see and he's afraid you might
remember."

"Nina, stop it! You're talking rubbish!"

Nina Blair paid no attention. "It's frightening to think
of a murderer at large in the hotel. It gives me palpita-
tions. I can feel my heart thudding against my ribs."

Reluctantly Maurice Blair pulled himself out of bed.
"I'll get you your heart pills, dear, and perhaps you could
take another sleeper."

"How can I possibly sleep tonight? You haven't contradicted me—about the danger, I mean. You think it was
someone in the hotel, don't you, Maurice?"

"Nina, I haven't the faintest idea!" Blair spoke sharply.
"At first I thought it was an accident, but as far as I can
make out the police consider that's unlikely because the
wound was so severe."

He padded into the bathroom to fetch his wife's pills
and, alone, drew a deep breath. He was sweating. If only

she'd stop talking about it, he thought. If only she'd been there, seen Mortlake, seen the back of his head . . . With an effort he controlled himself and returned to the bedroom.

"Here you are, dear. Take these."

Obediently Nina swallowed the capsules he brought and allowed him to plump her pillows and make her comfortable. It didn't occur to her to thank him. She seemed to be considering something. At last she said, "We must leave Wychwood House, Maurice. You'll have to explain to that policeman—Thorne, that's his name—that the strain is too much for me and we must go home."

Blair was taken by surprise. He sat heavily on the side of his bed, facing his wife. "We can't," he said. "He wouldn't let us. You perhaps, but I haven't even given a proper statement yet, and you can't travel without me."

"I shall speak to him myself," Nina said firmly.

"If you wish, dear." Blair sighed. He knew from experience that if he opposed the suggestion too violently Nina would become more obstinate. He thought for a moment. "Of course you must consider yourself first, but it'll be tough on the Kemptons if all their favourite guests desert them. And if you lead the way, others will follow."

"I suppose you're right, Maurice." Nina smothered a yawn. "I've never yet deserted anyone in trouble, and I'm very fond of the poor Kemptons. Perhaps we should stay a little."

Blair smiled. He felt overwhelmingly tired and he yearned for sleep. He was thankful to hear that Nina was beginning to sound drowsy. He got into bed and put out the light.

The lights had long been out in the Ravens' bedroom. They had talked for some time of the horrors of the day. It had been, they agreed, an unpleasant experience, so much more horrifying in reality than in a movie. But they were young and resilient and Roy Mortlake meant nothing to them personally. After a while they made love; then they slept.

# Chapter 10

It was only to be expected that the weekend would be miserable for everyone at Wychwood House. In spite of the Kemptons' efforts to maintain at least a semblance of normality in the running of the hotel, both guests and staff were tense. Inevitably the result was a series of small mishaps, unaccustomed lapses in the standard of service, unusually irritable responses when requests were not immediately gratified and a general air of apprehension.

The continuing police presence, as interviews continued and people were called to make formal statements, didn't help. Thorne and his fellow-officers did their best to keep a low profile, but the media men had no such inhibitions. The perimeter of the hotel's grounds was too long for any real security. The police did what they could, but soon reporters and photographers were at large, adding their share of unwonted excitement to the usually tranquil scene.

Another problem arose from the fact that visitors to Wychwood House often came and went at weekends. This meant that many of the visitors in residence had planned to depart, and others were due to arrive. The rooms had, in principle, been fully booked, but logistics—if not business prospects—were alleviated by the fact that the number of visitors expected to leave had been swollen by those who had no desire to remain in a place where one of their fellow-guests had almost certainly been murdered. And John Kempton had insisted that those due to arrive should be told of the situation by phone and given the option of cancelling their reservations; most had taken advantage of the warning.

"If you don't clear up this ghastly business pretty quickly, Superintendent," Helen Dearden said, "it'll be the end of the Wychwood House Hotel, at least for a season or two."

Thorne's smile was thin. "I'm aware of that, Mrs. Dearden." By now it was Sunday afternoon, and he was with Abbot in the room that served as their office, going through the list of guests wishing to leave, rapidly checking the names. He handed it back to her. "That's fine. As long as you make sure they've given full addresses in the register and get their phone numbers, they can go when they like—except for the Hurleys. Fortunately all the rest you've got on that list are sheep."

"Sheep?" Helen Dearden said, surprised.

Thorne cleared his throat as Abbot smothered his laughter with a cough. "Those who would seem to have absolutely no connection with the matter, as opposed to the—er—the others," he explained. "Miss Hurley was one of the first people on the scene, and thus she's a potentially important witness. Anyway, the Hurleys were booked for a couple of weeks, so they'll merely be continuing their intended holiday. Staying on shouldn't inconvenience them."

"I know, but the Canon—sheep or goat—he's particularly anxious to go." Mrs. Dearden kept her face straight. "He wasn't best pleased when I said I'd have to refer his departure plans to you, Superintendent."

"Really?" Thorne stroked his moustache reflectively. "If there's any difficulty, you tell him to come and see me, Mrs. Dearden. I'll deal with the matter."

"Thank you, Superintendent." Mrs. Dearden gave a small, almost conspiratorial, bow.

"Before you go, Mrs. Dearden, there's something I'd forgotten. Major Winston and his wife aren't on that list. I take it that means they don't want to leave. If so, that's a good thing, for I want a word with the Major."

"That may not be so easy, Superintendent."

"What?"

"I gather Major Winston went up to London for a few days on Friday morning. I didn't see him at meals, and I asked Lady Georgina. Apparently he's got some urgent business."

"Has he now." He paused. "Mrs. Dearden, I wonder if you'd find Lady Georgina and ask her to come and see me for a few minutes. More tactful than sending Sergeant Abbot, perhaps," he added.

"Of course, Superintendent."

"Nice woman, that," Thorne said as the door closed behind her. "I did have the odd doubt about her, but now I think her only motivation is to protect the Kemptons and the hotel. But that was a bad mistake on our part, Sergeant Abbot—forgetting about Winston. You remember what Fowler said?"

"Yes, sir," said Abbot, hastily searching his notes. Then, to change the subject, he asked, "Why do you think the Canon's so keen to leave, sir?"

Thorne grinned. "It'd be nice to know, wouldn't it? It could be quite natural, I suppose. But either he was lying through his teeth when he was talking to us earlier or he ought to get treated for his nerves. I've never seen a man more jumpy. However, we've only Latimer's word that the Canon was anywhere near the shrubbery. If we could get some confirmation it would be a big help."

"What'll you do if he takes his wife off and leaves his daughter behind, sir. You can't hold him."

"No. But from what I've seen of the family that would be a most unusual step for him to take—almost an admission he'd got an overwhelming reason to get away."

"And are you having Latimer in again now, sir?"

Thorne looked at his watch. "No, I think we'll see this Lady Georgina, have a quick tea and call it a day. After all, it is the Sabbath."

"No other reason, sir?" Abbot ventured.

"Yes. Mental indigestion." Thorne visibly relaxed. He stood up and spoke slowly and ruminatively as he paced the room. "In the last forty-eight hours or so we've acquired a great deal of information from the people here, much of it false or misleading, I suspect. We've got the result of the PM, and we know a good deal about Mortlake, partly thanks to the Canadians. As for friend Latimer, it may be irrelevant that the report on him's not much to his credit. Anyway, I need to read, mark, learn and inwardly digest all this. So do you, I suggest, Bill. And there'll be more bumpf waiting for us in Kidlington. So order up the tea."

Tea at Wychwood House was not a casual affair. A maid soon brought in a tray heavy with elegant sandwiches, scones and a variety of cakes. Thorne eyed it with pleasure and would have liked to give it the attention it merited, but time was passing, and the maid was closely followed by Lady Georgina. Regretfully, he turned his attention from the food to his new witness.

Lady Georgina was unmistakably nervous. She refused tea, and waited silently for the Superintendent to make the running. All she admitted in response to his questions was that her husband had gone to London on business—the trip had been planned a couple of days before. He had left early on Friday, and was probably staying at his club, though he would call at their London house for mail. She was certain he knew nothing of Mortlake's death. Nor for that matter did she—she'd scarcely met the man. She'd had a headache on Friday and had been mainly keeping to her room since.

Thorne demanded the name of the Major's club and verified their London address, then let her go. "Another little job for the Met," he said to Sergeant Abbot as he sorted his papers and put them in his briefcase.

"Damnation!" he exclaimed suddenly.

"Sir?" Abbot was startled.

"I've just found this." Thorne held up a book. "Cassandra Gray's latest novel. My wife made me promise I'd get her to autograph it. I completely forgot when we were interviewing her."

"Oh dear." Abbot had to bite his lip to prevent his laughter exploding. "There's always tomorrow, sir."

"Yes, you're right."

In the event they met Miss Gray in the hall as they were leaving. Wishing Abbot elsewhere, Thorne stopped her. For once his seeming diffidence was genuine, but quite unnecessary. Cassandra Gray was happy to sign her book for him.

"For my wife," Thorne corrected her hurriedly, with less than his usual tact. "Miranda Thorne."

"Of course! I should have known, but I didn't make the connection, Superintendent." Miss Gray smiled with delight. "I met your wife the Saturday I believe you had lunch here. I was doing one of her acrostics at the time and she introduced herself."

"I know, Miss Gray. She told me."

"I'd have liked to talk to her more, but then Mrs. Kempton came into the lounge. She was unwell, almost fainting, and we had to help her."

"I see," said Thorne slowly, frowning. "My wife didn't mention that."

Seeing Thorne's frown and sensing his interest, Miss Gray began to make light of the incident. "Oh, it was nothing, Superintendent. A moment's dizziness, no more."

"Probably," Thorne agreed. He thanked her profusely as she signed her book, and added a dedication to Miranda. "That was virtue rewarded," he added to Abbot when they were on their way, "or it might be."

Abbot looked blank. "I don't quite follow, sir."

George Thorne didn't explain. He was busy on the car radio, getting patched through to his wife. Abbot ostentatiously concentrated on his driving, but listened hard. Able to hear only one side of the conversation, he learnt little. When the call had ended he cast a sideways glance at his superior; the Superintendent was stroking his moustache and frowning again.

"So far so good," he said suddenly. "We'll try Mrs. Dearden next. She'll have left Wychwood House by now but we must have her home number."

"The list's in your briefcase, sir," Abbot said and waited, hopeful that the call to the receptionist would be more enlightening.

"Just a small point, Mrs. Dearden," Thorne said, after apologizing for bothering her at home. "Could you tell me exactly what time of day it was that Mr. Mortlake phoned to ask if you could accommodate him?"

It seemed that Mrs. Dearden could and would, and Abbot was left in the annoying position of watching Thorne nod to himself with satisfaction—just like that toy dog on the rear shelf of the car in front, thought Abbot—while he himself remained in the dark. He hooted loudly and unnecessarily at the car to show his disapproval, but the Superintendent had said goodbye to Mrs. Dearden and was signing off.

"It looks as if Rose Kempton knew Mortlake *before* he came to Wychwood House." Thorne's voice was carefully neutral. "I've been checking the time sequence, Sergeant. Mortlake phoned on the Saturday morning to see if he could make a booking. Mrs. Kempton hears about it, and promptly almost faints. It could be coincidence, but I doubt it, I doubt it."

Abbot did his best to sound equally impersonal. "Which means she would have lied to us, sir. And John Kempton? You said you thought he was hiding something."

"John Kempton, too," Thorne agreed. "And Paul, I suspect." He sighed. "Too bad," he said reflectively, and closed his eyes.

Miranda Thorne sighed as she raised her head from the puzzle she was attempting to devise. "I can't concentrate," she said. Then, "I wish someone else was in charge of this inquiry, other than you, George."

"So do I, in a way." Thorne was grim. "It's not pleasant having to suspect one's friends; on the other hand I'm likely to give them a fairer deal than another chap who didn't know them." He pushed himself out of his favourite armchair and wandered over to the window. Miranda, he noted absently, had mown the grass.

"There's no possibility of accident, George?"

Reluctantly Thorne turned back to face his wife. "Miranda, you know better than that. The PM report was definite. There was no water in the lungs. Mortlake was dead before he entered the water. We think we've found the place he was killed, and he didn't crawl from there into the pool after he was dead. What's more, we've got the weapon; there were bits of his head on that bottle of lime juice we found in the shrubbery. No, it's murder, without a doubt."

"I shouldn't have thought a lime juice bottle would necessarily kill anyone."

"It was full, and a full bottle's surprisingly heavy. Held by the neck it makes a perfectly weighted club, when you come to think of it."

"So it was murder. And premeditated?"

"In my opinion, yes. At least I think the killer intended to kill his victim. Whether he actually planned it as it worked out, I'm not sure."

Miranda frowned, putting aside her pad of paper and picking up some knitting. "You mean he found the bottle by chance and seized his opportunity? He didn't hide it somewhere beforehand, or carry it with him? That doesn't suggest premeditation. Anyway, how would the killer know where to hide it? How would he know Mortlake's route in advance?"

Thorne shrugged. "That's all irrelevant, Miranda, except perhaps from a jury's point of view. I think someone wanted Mortlake dead."

He paused and then went on, as if visualizing the scene in his mind's eye. "I think that same someone—the killer—knew about Mortlake's habit of a pre-breakfast walk and followed him. I think the killer picked up a weapon—the bottle—probably behind the bar by the pool, realized that Mortlake would be returning through the shrubbery and waited for him there. I think he persuaded Mortlake to look at something on or under the hydrangea bush and then—then just let him have it on the back of the head."

"So it must have been someone Mortlake knew?"

"That's a reasonable assumption." Thorne was again silent for a moment before he continued more slowly. "Now this is where I believe things went wrong—for the killer, I mean. I believe he intended to knock Mortlake out—preferably without breaking the skin—and push him into the pool to drown. A not unreasonable accident, with the wet leaves about, and all. What he didn't know was that Mortlake had an abnormally thin skull. How could he? No one knew—probably not even Mortlake himself—till we got the PM report. I'd guess that it was then the killer panicked. When he saw the mess he'd made of Mortlake's head, he threw away the bottle and ran."

"And someone else—a third party—saw him and

dragged the body into the water? Just to confuse things?"
Miranda sounded somewhat sceptical.

Thorne nodded. "And why not? Throwing the bottle
away into the shrubbery was an irrational act—an act of
panic, if you like—on the part of the murderer. Can you
see him doing anything else after that, but bolt?"

"Oh dear! George, you're making it look bad for the
Kemptons. They're so devoted to one another. If John—or
Paul—"

Miranda paused, distressed. Then she went on hurriedly. "No, no, I can't really see it . . . Anyway, there
must be a lot more to learn about Mortlake's background.
For instance, what about his family? Was he ever married
or divorced or anything?"

"We're looking into all that, Miranda. The damned
civil servants in the Registrar's Office in St. Catherine's
House and the Divorce Registry in Somerset House don't
work on Sundays. But officers from the Met'll be along at
both places first thing in the morning to do a routine
check on Mortlake and his marital status. And we've put
in the usual request to the RCMP, too. If there are any
results, I'll probably be going up to London tomorrow
with Sergeant Abbot, as soon as I've dictated a report and
had a word with the Chief Constable."

Miranda made no comment. She merely said, "To
confirm, George. You think it's a—what used they to call
it—a true bill, didn't they?—against one or other of the
Kemptons, I mean?" The question came out rather for-
mally, as if Miranda were accusing her husband. She
realized this, and added, "I'm sorry, George."

"I know how you feel." Thorne shook his head sadly.
"But cheer up. Lots of people have secrets in their past,
things they'd prefer weren't known. It doesn't make them
all guilty of murder."

"Like the young man who calls himself Tom Latimer?"

"Quite. His dabs on that ashtray confirmed what I
suspected. He's got a record, and he's done time—for
violence. I remember the case vaguely, and I hope to see
the officer who was in charge of it tomorrow, too. Then
there's this chap Winston, who seems to have made himself scarce at the crucial moment. His wife was clearly

lying; I've got a shrewd suspicion she's no more idea where he is than I have. We'll have to look into that in London tomorrow, too. Which reminds me, it's getting late, and I need an early start."

Miranda finished her row, folded her knitting and put it beside her. "Tea or whisky?" she asked.

"Tea, tonight, perhaps."

"I'll go and make it. Then bed."

"And don't worry too much about the Kemptons, love," George Thorne said as she bustled out to the kitchen. "There are still a lot of other runners. The damned thing's far from over."

# Introducing the first and only complete hardcover collection of Agatha Christie's mysteries

Now you can enjoy the
greatest mysteries ever written
in a magnificent
Home Library Edition.

# Discover Agatha Christie's world of mystery, adventure and intrigue

Agatha Christie's timeless tales of mystery and suspense offer something for every reader—mystery fan or not—young and old alike. And now, you can build a complete hardcover library of her world-famous mysteries by subscribing to The Agatha Christie Mystery Collection.

This exciting Collection is your passport to a world where mystery reigns supreme. Volume after volume, you and your family will enjoy mystery reading at its very best.

You'll meet Agatha Christie's world-famous detectives like Hercule Poirot, Jane Marple, and the likeable Tommy and Tuppence Beresford.

In your readings, you'll visit Egypt, Paris, England and other exciting destinations where murder is always on the itinerary. And wherever you travel, you'll become deeply involved in some of the most ingenious and diabolical plots ever invented... "cliff-hangers" that only Dame Agatha could create!

It all adds up to mystery reading that's so good... it's almost criminal. And it's yours every month with The Agatha Christie Mystery Collection.

**Solve the greatest mysteries of all time.** The Collection contains all of Agatha Christie's classic works including *Murder on the Orient Express, Death on the Nile, And Then There Were None, The ABC Murders* and her ever-popular whodunit, *The Murder of Roger Ackroyd.*

Each handsome hardcover volume is Smythe sewn and printed on high quality acid-free paper so it can withstand even the most murderous treatment. Bound in Sussex-blue simulated leather with gold titling, The Agatha Christie Mystery Collection will make a tasteful addition to your living room, or den.

**Ride the Orient Express for 10 days without obligation.** To introduce you to the Collection, we're inviting you to examine the classic mystery, *Murder on the Orient Express*, without risk or obligation. If you're not completely satisfied, just return it within 10 days and owe nothing.

However, if you're like the millions of other readers who love Agatha Christie's thrilling tales of mystery and suspense, keep *Murder on the Orient Express* and pay just $9.95 plus postage and handling.

You will then automatically receive future volumes once a month as they are published on a fully returnable, 10-day free-examination basis. No minimum purchase is required, and you may cancel your subscription at any time.

This unique collection is not sold in stores. It's available only through this special offer. So don't miss out, begin your subscription now. Just mail this card today.

# BUSINESS REPLY MAIL

FIRST CLASS    PERMIT NO. 2154    HICKSVILLE, N.Y.

Postage will be paid by addressee:

The Agatha Christie
Mystery Collection
Bantam Books
P.O. Box 956
Hicksville, N.Y. 11802

# Chapter 11

By the late afternoon of the following day, not many guests remained at the Wychwood House Hotel. Cars had departed hurriedly as soon as the police gave permission, and there had been no influx of new visitors. For those who had stayed, either willingly or because Superintendent Thorne had requested their continued presence, the hotel could have become an unhappy refuge.

The situation was saved by the Fowlers—William and Anne. Today was their fortieth wedding anniversary and, having decided that Mortlake's death should not interfere with their plans for a champagne reception before dinner for their family, friends in the neighbourhood and old acquaintances who happened to be staying in the hotel, they had generously invited all the remaining guests. Characteristically, though their reasons were partly selfish—they wanted their party to be a success—their main motivation was a wish to give the Kemptons every possible support and encouragement in these trying days, a desire shared by the entire staff.

In his kitchen, Felix, the chef, was putting as much enthusiasm into the preparations for what he insisted on calling the Fowlers' *vin d'honneur* as he would have done for a full-scale banquet. "They don't want a cake," he said. "*Alors*, no cake. But I have made them a *tarte*, a big—how do you say?—a big pastry flan, a big open pie in the shape of a heart, with a delectable savoury filling. It will be the centrepiece of the *vin d'honneur*. Go and look, Mrs.

Kempton. They cannot refuse it, not without offending me deeply." Felix bowed his head in a Gallic gesture of despair.

"Mr. and Mrs. Fowler would never do that," Rose Kempton said quickly.

Rose was pale, but outwardly composed. She had ceased to think of what might happen to her family, to contemplate what was happening to the hotel. She had found that so long as she kept herself busy with her usual chores plus some additional, unnecessary tasks she could at least maintain some kind of front. No one expected her to appear exactly carefree in the present circumstances.

From the kitchens Rose went on a tour of inspection. At this time many of the visitors were in their rooms preparing for the Fowlers' party, but in the lounge Cassandra Gray, already changed, was absorbed in a cross-word puzzle and Lady Georgina Winston, in a black velvet cocktail dress, was idly turning the pages of a magazine.

"Is there any hope that the Major will be returning for this evening's party, Lady Georgina?" Rose asked.

"No, no. I shouldn't think so, not now." Lady Georgina forced herself to smile; she had not as yet quite abandoned the pretence that she knew of her husband's whereabouts and his plans. "Such a pity," she added brightly. "He'll be sorry to miss it."

Rose nodded her understanding. In the hall she met Canon and Mrs. Hurley. She would have passed them with a casual good-evening, but the Canon stopped her.

"Mrs. Kempton, perhaps you can tell me. Has that Superintendent been here today?"

"I don't think so, Canon. No. I've not seen Superintendent Thorne, though the police are still around the hotel, I'm afraid."

"But that's disgraceful! They say we're to stay on here, whether we like it or not, and then the only man who can release us, as it were, doesn't even bother to turn up. Why? What on earth are they doing, we ask. Are we to sit, twiddling our thumbs, and await their pleasure?"

"Peter!" Margaret Hurley protested mildly.

Her husband paid no attention. "Mrs. Kempton, we come here once a year expecting a quiet, relaxing holiday, and we find ourselves in the middle of this—this affair, this muddle. It's too bad."

"I'm very sorry, Canon—Mrs. Hurley." Rose looked from one to the other. "Very sorry. What—what more can I say?"

"I don't know," said the Canon reasonably. But he was exasperated enough to add, "It's not good enough, you know."

"Well, it damn well has to be, Canon Hurley!"

Rose's temper had snapped at last. She swept past the Hurleys, along the corridor and into the dining-room, part of which had been closed so that it would not look too empty. The tables were already laid for dinner. The Fowlers' own table—for themselves and their son and daughter-in-law from London, who were staying overnight—was set in a window alcove, and its flower arrangement was especially fine. Rose's eyes filled with tears of self-pity as the ruby colours of the blooms reminded her of the length and apparent success of the Fowlers' marriage, but she quickly blinked them away when she heard an anxious voice inquire, "Mrs. Kempton—Mrs. Kempton, are you all right?"

"Mr. Blair! I—I'm fine. Just something in my eye and—and you startled me. I didn't know there was anyone else here."

"I'm sorry. Didn't you see me? I've been looking for my reading glasses. I thought I might have left them in here after lunch."

"Oh, I'm sorry. Did you find them?"

"No, unfortunately not." Maurice Blair smiled deprecatingly. "I hope they turn up. I'm always mislaying them, and Nina gets so annoyed with me. She thinks I do it on purpose."

"Perhaps they're in one of the lounges," Rose said hopefully, and watched with sympathy as Blair went off to search. Nina Blair, she thought, couldn't be the easiest of women to live with.

Satisfied with the dinner arrangements, Rose went along to the lounge where the reception was to be held. It was a big room, used mainly for such functions. A long table had been placed across one end to carry the cocktail food—smoked salmon, caviare, tiny *vot-au-vents* and so on—as well as act as a bar; Felix's *pièce de résistance* was already in place. There were flowers everywhere here, too, and the atmosphere was festive.

Anne Fowler turned to greet Rose. "I just came to have a peep," she said, "and everything looks wonderful. Felix has outdone himself. I've never seen anything quite like that heart."

"He was determined to do something special for you, and you said you'd prefer not to have a cake. I gather it's got a special filling." Rose smiled, hesitated, then added, "All of us here at Wychwood House wanted you and Mr. Fowler to have a happy day."

"It *is* being a happy day." Impulsively Anne Fowler went across to Rose, and put an arm around her to give her a quick hug. "My dear, I know you're going through a bad patch at present, but it'll pass. These things always do."

Rose was warmed by Anne Fowler's gesture of affection. A little more relaxed now, she followed the older woman from the room. She herself wasn't looking forward to the festivities, but she hoped, for the Fowlers' sake and for the sake of all their guests, that they would be successful, in spite of the miserable circumstances.

William and Anne Fowler stood, with their son and daughter-in-law, in a formal if somewhat ragged receiving line. None of their guests grudged them this celebration, though some found it difficult not to envy them the reason for it.

John Kempton was wondering if he and Rose would ever be able to celebrate their own fortieth wedding anniversary; Rose herself had no such hope. Lady Georgina Winston was fearful that her marriage—such as it was—had already ended. Alice Hurley was afraid that she would never be married—to Tom Latimer or anyone else. Since the murder Tom seemed to have been avoiding her, but she found it hard to believe that in his eyes she had been merely a "one night stand"; she shivered at the phrase, then, in spite of herself, smiled at her memories.

As for the rest of the guests, they were content to drink and eat and chat, their thoughts mainly far from love

and marriage. Indeed, Canon Hurley, when questioned
by Mrs. Blair, found himself unable to remember the date
of his wedding.

"Perhaps they weren't. Perhaps he and Mrs. H have
been living in sin," Polly Raven whispered to Vern when
she overheard this conversation. Vern, delighted at the
suggestion, threw up his eyes in mock horror.

Cassandra Gray, standing nearby, had sharp ears too,
and she commented to Polly, "That would surprise me,
though Canons are only human, and almost everyone has
a secret, you know." Then, grinning at the young couple's
startled expression, she wandered away.

At the appropriate moment, when the waiters had
made sure that everyone's glass was full, the Fowlers' son
banged on the table for silence. He made a pleasant, if
obvious, speech, hoping that he and his wife would one
day be taking part in a similar celebration, and proposed
his parents' health. Tim Railton, a lawyer from Colombury,
took the opportunity to thank the Fowlers on behalf of
their guests, remarking that it was he who had been
instrumental in recommending Wychwood House to William and Anne many years ago. William then thanked his
guests in two or three brief sentences, and Felix's pastry
heart was cut and distributed. The party resumed until
people began to drift away to dinner.

Probably it was the champagne, or the sharing of a
pleasurable occasion, or the fact that the remaining tables
had been compressed more closely together than usual,
but when John Kempton glanced into the room a while
later, he was glad to find that the party atmosphere had
continued during dinner; his visitors seemed more at ease,
with themselves and with each other, than at any time
since Mortlake's death. He exchanged a glance with Dr.
Band and his wife, who had also been guests at the reception, and had stayed on for dinner with the Railtons; he
felt certain that the same thought had occurred to them.

People were noticeably less reserved and more friendly.
Cassandra Gray, noting that the Major was still missing,
had invited Lady Georgina to share her table. Mrs. Blair
went so far as to pass Canon Hurley a pepper-mill when
he couldn't immediately attract the attention of a waiter.

Vern Raven, who had travelled in Scandinavia as a student, met Anne Fowler's eyes and raised his glass to offer her a traditional Norwegian *Skol*. Several others copied him.

"A good day and a very good party." William Fowler summed up as he and Anne went to bed. "Let's hope things will turn out as well for everyone at Wychwood House."

Fowler's wish was not to be fulfilled. By midnight several inhabitants of the Wychwood House Hotel had become ill. Vern Raven was among the first; Polly was less sympathetic than she might have been.

"Too much champagne," she said firmly. "I said you were drinking too much, Vern."

"I had no more than you," her husband protested untruthfully.

"Then why do I feel fine?" Polly demanded.

Vern Raven had no answer. Secretly he believed that Polly could well be right, and anyway he had no wish to argue. He was sick to his stomach. Making an incomprehensible noise, he dashed for the bathroom as his insides cramped.

Georgina Winston had also attributed her symptoms to too much champagne because she could think of no other reason. She felt dreadful. Her head was splitting, she was suffering from internal cramps and she wanted to vomit, but couldn't. Never one to bear pain, physical or mental, stoically, she groaned loudly, and eventually Cassandra Gray knocked on her door to inquire if she needed help.

"I've got the most bloody awful hangover you can imagine," Lady Georgina said resentfully.

"Are you sure it *is* a hangover?" asked Miss Gray, who had drunk sparingly. "I'm a little queasy myself. It might be something we've eaten."

Anne Fowler, who was always abstemious, was having much the same thought. She felt distinctly unwell. Sliding quietly out of bed so as not to disturb her husband who was snoring gently, she hurried to the bathroom where she vomited. Afterwards she felt better and returned to bed. By now William was awake. There was obviously nothing wrong with him and, as Anne seemed to have recovered, they talked for a while, then slept.

The Blairs were not so fortunate. They were both really ill. Nina was in bed. She complained of headache and cramps and nausea and was sweating heavily, her pretty, petulant face flushed to an unbecoming pink. Maurice ran between the bathroom, where he had to attend to his own needs, and his wife, bringing her indigestion tablets, cold towels for her head, thermometer, eau-de-Cologne, paper handkerchiefs. When she found she had a fever she demanded that he telephone for Dr. Band.

"In a minute," Maurice said. "In a minute, dear. I—I—" Hand clamped over his mouth, he made a dash for the bathroom. "Coming, coming," he said a little later as Nina called impatiently, but it was some while before he actually appeared, whey-faced and unsteady on his feet, and went to the telephone.

Canon Hurley was equally unwell. Staggering back from his bathroom, he fell against the end of the bed and slipped to the ground. His wife made an effort to lift him, but she was not a strong woman and the Canon seemed unable to help her. He was breathing hard and sweating, and complained of dizziness—symptoms similar to those being suffered in various degrees by others in the hotel.

Margaret Hurley hurried to the adjoining room. There her daughter lay awake, thinking of Tom Latimer and wondering if her affair was really over before it had scarcely begun. Like her mother, Alice hadn't felt in the least ill, but the sight of her father on the floor frightened her.

"Mother, we must get a doctor," she said decidedly. "We'll get Father into bed, then I'll phone down to the night porter. I expect he'll call Dr. Band, but we'd better leave it to him."

"I'm sure you're right, dear," Margaret Hurley agreed after a glance at her husband; the Hurleys didn't send for doctors lightly, but this was clearly a crisis. "I've never seen him in this state before."

Between them the two women managed to lift the Canon back on to his bed and make him comfortable. He had apparently recovered a little and seemed half asleep.

His wife had second thoughts about sending for a doctor but Alice insisted. To her relief the night porter answered his phone before it had rung twice. He assured her that he would get Dr. Band as soon as possible. She was too preoccupied to notice that his voice sounded strained.

The porter put down his receiver and stared at it, as if daring it to ring again. He had answered it three times in about as many minutes, Miss Gray speaking for Lady Georgina Winston, young Mrs. Raven and now the Hurleys. All had made requests for doctors.

Reluctantly the night porter decided that before phoning Dr. Band he would have to disturb John Kempton. Something was seriously wrong and the boss must know.

# Chapter 12

It was six-thirty in the morning before Dr. Band, tired and more than a little worried, returned home. It was too late, he decided, to go back to bed. His wife called out to him and he put his head around their bedroom door.

"I heard you come in," she said. "I was awake. What's the situation like at Wychwood House, Dick?"

"Not good. I've put on the kettle. I'll bring us our early morning cuppas and tell you about it."

Minutes later, when he brought in the tea, Mary Band said, "Poor Kemptons, as if a murder on the premises wasn't enough. And now this—whatever this is—"

"It looks like a straightforward case of food poisoning. There's an overall pattern, but it's variable. Some people's symptoms are much more acute than others. Some don't seem to have suffered any ill-effects; all the Kemptons are fine, for instance. For that matter, so are we, though we were at the Fowlers' party and stayed on to dinner at the hotel."

"Those are the possibilities—contaminated food at either the party or the dinner afterwards?"

"Judging from the time the victims began to develop their symptoms, yes. There's also the point that none of the staff have been affected, at least none of those who sleep there. We'll know more later, of course. I've taken some samples, but I'll have to report the whole thing. The health authorities'll get involved, and there'll be a proper inquiry. A hotel's a public place, you know."

"I see," said Mary slowly as she grasped the full

enormity of what had struck Wychwood House. "And the
Fowlers? How are they?" she asked.

"Mrs. Fowler was slightly ill, but he felt no effects at
all. Nor did their son, though the daughter-in-law was
unsure. Which reminds me—it might be a good idea to
call the Railtons and see if they're all right."

Mary said, "I'm going to get up and cook you some
breakfast. You'll be going back to Wychwood House later,
I suppose?"

"Mrs. Blair would demand my presence, quite apart
from anyone else," Band said ruefully. "In fact, she's been
pretty bad and so has her husband, by the look of him,
though it's she who makes the fuss and gets all the attention. Anyway, I want to keep an eye on some of the
others—Canon Hurley and the young American boy and
two or three more. And, apart from my patients, there'll
be the health people to cope with later on—and Superintendent Thorne, I guess."

"Thorne?" Mary Band had pulled on a robe and was
feeling for her slippers. She looked up sharply. "Dick,
you're suspicious, aren't you? That this may not be what it
seems, I mean."

Band shook his head. "Not really. But you yourself
mentioned the murder. I'd certainly have accepted it at its
face value as food poisoning if it hadn't been for Roy
Mortlake's death. As it is—"

"You can't help wondering?"

"That's right. And I expect George Thorne will have
the same thoughts."

"Poor Kemptons," Mary Band said again. "For their
sakes, let's hope all the suspicions are unfounded and it's
merely a question of tainted smoked salmon or something
like that."

John Kempton, facing one of a hotel keeper's constant
nightmares, was as anxious as anyone to discover the
source of the illness. He started in the obvious place, the
kitchens, and with the obvious people, the staff who came
into contact with the food. Monsieur Lechat was not pleased.

"First Dr. Band comes with his questions and his little
bottles wanting samples of my food," he declared. "Then

you. My kitchens are spotless. I told the doctor and I tell you. Let anyone come, see for themselves. Everywhere is hygiene. And my staff, I watch them all the time. If I catch someone returning from the toilet and not scrubbing his hands I make big fuss."

"Felix, we know how careful you are and we appreciate it," Kempton said, "but something went wrong yesterday, and we've got to discover what it was as soon as possible—preferably before the health investigators arrive. I have the dinner menu, of course, but I'll need a list of everything prepared for the Fowlers' reception, and a note of what's left."

"These kitchens—they are like an operating room in a hospital. They could not be cleaner if—"

"Felix!" Kempton interrupted the irate Frenchman. "I'm not accusing you of anything—no one is. I'm asking for your help. I need it. Mrs. Kempton needs it. Please cooperate with us."

Thus appealed to, Lechat was fully ready to help, and his care and efficiency proved a bonus. He knew what had been eaten by the guests both at the Fowlers' party and at dinner, what had been finished by the hotel staff, what had been put by in the refrigerator for possible later use.

By the time Superintendent Thorne and Sergeant Abbot arrived at Wychwood House, Kempton had been able to establish certain pertinent facts. Whatever had caused the outbreak had been consumed by the guests either at the party or at the dinner. No one else—no members of the staff, for instance—had been taken ill, regardless of what they had eaten. And since only some of the guests had been victims, suspicion would seem to rest particularly on the dinner, where the need to choose from a menu would more readily enable some to escape; at the party, with a wide variety of cocktail food, it was on the whole more likely that everyone, or almost everyone, would have eaten contaminated food.

"At least that's how I see it," said Kempton. He was in his office with Thorne and Abbot, and they had just been joined by Dr. Band, who was busy examining menus and waiters' orders.

"You may well be right," said the doctor. "What

needs to be done is to discover exactly who had what for dinner. For example, if only the sick had sole, then the problem's half-way solved, as sole wasn't served at the party. These waiters' chits only say what was served at each table; they don't put names to the eaters, as it were." He looked hopefully at Thorne.

"Not really our job," the Superintendent remarked. "It's a matter for the health people. Still, we'll do what we can."

"They'll be along. I told you I've reported the outbreak to Oxford. Sorry, John," Band added to Kempton, "but I had no choice."

"I realize that." Kempton nodded grimly. "But the more I can find out before they come, the better I'll be able to cope with them. If you'd check with the patients you're going to see now, Dick, I'd be grateful. Meanwhile I'll try to discover what the rest had for dinner, and—"

"No. Not immediately," Thorne interrupted. "I've got to talk to you privately first, John—and to Rose. It's important. But perhaps Sergeant Abbot could . . ."

Glancing at his sergeant, Thorne appeared to hesitate as if leaving the decision to Bill Abbot. But Abbot knew the Superintendent better than that. This was undoubtedly his cue to depart and make himself useful elsewhere.

He stood up. "Yes, sir," he said smartly, wondering what the Superintendent was up to now, and what rules he might have decided to bend.

In their private sitting-room John and Rose Kempton sat side by side opposite Thorne. Rose seemed lost in a daze of unhappiness, but John was ready to be aggressive.

"What's this about then, George?" he said. "Not more trouble? We've enough here already, you know."

Thorne wasn't prepared to mince words. He said, "Yes, and some of it's of your own making. You lied to me. You told me Roy Mortlake was a stranger to you. You didn't bother to mention he was Rose's husband."

"Ex-husband," Kempton corrected.

"You each made an official statement. Do either of you wish to correct them?" Thorne looked at Rose, who shook her head hopelessly.

Kempton intervened. "All right, all right. But for God's sake, George, be human. I give you my word neither of us had anything to do with Mortlake's death."

Thorne appeared unmoved. "You had a motive," he said.

"No! Mortlake turned up out of the blue. He was as surprised to see Rose as she was to see him. Sure, they were married years ago. He gave her a hell of a time and then deserted her. But that was years ago. Why should we want to kill him now? All his death's done is help to ruin the hotel."

"Was he blackmailing you?" Thorne's question was blunt.

"No. What for? How could he?"

Thorne didn't answer Kempton directly. "There's evidence he was throwing his weight around. What about the fight with Paul?"

"It wasn't a fight. And it was based on a misunderstanding. No one's ever denied it."

"And you say you had no reason to wish him dead?"

"Yes. Yes, we did." Rose spoke quickly, anticipating John's denial. "It's no use," she warned him. "George knows. Can't you see he knows—everything?"

For a long minute there was silence in the room. Then John Kempton said, "All right! The man was a shit! Who but a shit would prostitute his wife for his own ends? I hated him, hated his guts for what he'd done to Rose. Who wouldn't in my place?"

The Superintendent, who privately had a good deal of sympathy with John Kempton, remained impassive. Rose was wrong. He knew a lot, but apparently not "everything," though he was learning fast. For example, the fact that Mortlake had forced Rose to become a prostitute before deserting her did not appear in any records. Thorne paused, planning his next move. Then he said persuasively, "You're sure you didn't kill him, John? It might have been an accident."

"No, damn you! And I don't know who did, but I wish him luck."

"What about you, Rose?"

"Don't be absurd!" John Kempton said roughly.

Rose shook her head and spoke quite quietly. "No. I didn't kill him, George."

"Why did you never divorce him?"

After those that had preceded it, the question sounded casual, unimportant even. Its results were all that Thorne had expected. John Kempton made an inarticulate noise at the back of his throat as if he were about to choke. Rose simply buried her face in her hands and wept. The Superintendent waited.

"John didn't know till now," Rose said at last through her fingers.

"But why no divorce?" Thorne persisted.

Rose raised her head and shrugged. She had recovered her composure and seemed prepared to face the worst, though she kept her eyes firmly on Thorne and didn't look at John. "Roy had gone, disappeared," she said. "I had no idea how to set about a divorce, and no money for one. Anyway, at the time it seemed—unnecessary. Then I met John. We lived together. He asked me to marry him, but I refused. I said once was enough. When I got pregnant he insisted. I'd never told him I'd been married to Roy, and I couldn't tell him then. There wouldn't have been time to get a divorce before the baby was born and—and I was afraid I might lose him—John, I mean."

"I was pressing her," Kempton said gruffly. "I didn't want my son to be illegitimate. I know a lot of people don't consider it important these days, but it was different when I was a nipper. I suffered from not having a proper dad."

"I'm sorry," Rose said.

"It wasn't your fault, love. It was that damned—" He stopped. "What happens now?" he said to Thorne. "Are you going to have Rose up for bigamy? Or will it be both of us?"

"I very much doubt it. I imagine the whole thing can be sorted out." Thorne stood up abruptly. "Now I must go and see how Sergeant Abbot's getting on."

With a nod of farewell he left them. As he closed the door behind him he saw that John Kempton was on his knees beside Rose's chair, his arms around her, his whole attention concentrated on consoling her, making her realize that his love for her hadn't changed. But Thorne's own expression was bleak as he wondered what his superiors would say about murder suspects with such an excellent motive.

The Superintendent had no wish to interfere with Abbot's culinary inquiries, so he went along to the reception desk. As it was Tuesday and Helen Dearden's day off, Paul Kempton was on duty. He greeted Thorne with a marked lack of enthusiasm.

"Something I can do for you, Superintendent?"

"Yes. Could you get hold of Tom Latimer and tell him to come to my interview room."

"He's not here today."

"You mean it's his day off? He'll be somewhere on the premises."

"No. He went up to London early this morning."

"What? Not another! I never gave him permission."

Paul looked puzzled. "Superintendent, you weren't here yesterday. Tom asked Dad, and Dad said he could go for the day. Why not? Your orders were that people weren't to leave for good."

"And he chooses this moment—in the middle of a murder investigation, and just when a lot of the guests here have got some sort of poisoning!" Thorne was angry, mostly with himself; he knew he should have taken precautions against Latimer trying to bolt. "What I said was that no one was to leave without my permission."

"Tom hasn't *left*, Superintendent. He's gone to London for the day, that's all. I told you he went early. You know he rooms with the head gardener, so if he went straight off he wouldn't have heard about the poisoning. He'll be back tonight."

"Let's hope so." Thorne was curt. For a moment he wondered whether he should start the routine wheels in motion and get on to the Met, but he decided against any action, at least until he saw whether Latimer did reappear by next morning.

Turning away from Paul Kempton, the Superintendent nearly bumped into Dr. Band. The doctor waved a piece of paper at him. "Here are the details of my patients' food intake yesterday. Not uninteresting, I think, though in a negative way."

"Dad'll want to see that," Paul Kempton said at once.

"We'll let him have a copy of all our findings in due course," Thorne said shortly.

He took Band by the elbow and steered him across the hall into a lounge. They sat on a sofa while Thorne studied the results of the doctor's inquiries. They were, as Band had said, not uninteresting.

The two young Americans and Lady Georgina Winston had chosen nearly identical meals for dinner; the only difference was that Polly Raven had refused the fish course. The three Hurleys, however, had eaten the fish, and so had Maurice Blair, but not Nina. Another possibly suspect dish was the mushroom savoury, but Canon Hurley, who disliked mushrooms and never ate them, had, appropriately enough, preferred "angels on horseback." The net result of all this seemed to be that both the fish and the mushrooms were exonerated, and there was no other sign of correlation between the choice of food at dinner and the incidence of sickness.

Dr. Band said, "It's my opinion that the dinner can be eliminated, and that leaves the party. Incidentally, it more or less has to be one or the other because Tom Railton and his wife were both slightly unwell in the night. I've just phoned them."

Thorne nodded. "I agree. It looks like the party, which is a pity. People'll never remember what kind of bits and pieces they ate."

"I know. My lot were terribly vague, no help whatsoever." Band glanced at his watch. "I must be off, or I'll be late for my surgery. If the health people ever arrive they can contact me there. In the meantime, maybe Bill Abbot will have come up with something."

Abbot's report, however, merely served to confirm the conclusion reached by Thorne and Dr. Band—and earlier by John Kempton. There could have been nothing wrong with the dinner. As for the party, it was impossible to say. Everyone recalled having been served a piece of the big pastry heart that had been the centrepiece of the table, but apart from that memories were sketchy. No one could be exact, and no further conclusions could be drawn.

"Do you really think this poisoning could be anything other than chance, sir?" Sergeant Abbot asked as he drove the Superintendent back to Kidlington. "It's so indiscriminate, and there haven't been any fatalities or even near-fatalities. In fact, no one's been really ill."

"Certainly if it was a murder attempt—to get rid of someone who saw something they shouldn't, say—it was a pretty inefficient one," Thorne said. "I dislike coincidence, as you know, Sergeant Abbot, but I'm forced to admit it looks unlikely that Mortlake's death and this food business are connected." With this the Superintendent relapsed into silence.

Superintendent Thorne's view of coincidence was not shared by the media. Both television and radio news that evening happily linked the murder and the poisoning, and next day the events at Wychwood House made a splash in the tabloids. Headlines such as "Hotel Killer Strikes Again" and "More Victims at Horror Hotel" didn't please the Kemptons, or their staff, or their guests—or the police.

# Chapter 13

Tom Latimer glanced into the lounge, which was empty, and the dining-room, where two or three guests were having breakfast. Alice Hurley was not among them. Latimer made for the service staircase, and took the steps two at a time. As he hurried along the bedroom floor corridor Alice emerged from her room.

"Miss Hurley!"

Alice had turned away as she shut the door and hadn't seen Latimer, but she recognized his voice. For a second she wondered how to respond. Then, "Yes," she said coldly.

"Alice." Tom Latimer came up to her and took her by the hands. "You're all right? Felix said one of the Hurleys was very ill and I was afraid it was you."

Partly mollified, Alice replied, "No. It was my father."

"But you have been ill? You don't look well."

"I'm fine. I wasn't affected. All that's wrong with me is lack of sleep. I can't have eaten whatever upset people."

"I knew nothing about it till this morning. I left early yesterday and didn't get back till late. I had to go up to London to see my lawyer."

"Your what?"

Latimer swore softly and hastily released Alice's hands. "I can't explain now, Alice," he said softly. Then more loudly, "Of course, I could be wrong, Miss Hurley, but it looks to me like a slow puncture." He drew back a pace. "Good morning, Mrs. Hurley. I was just telling Miss Hurley I think there may be a slow puncture in one of the rear tyres of your car."

"Oh dear! Well, I can't bother the Canon with that at the moment. He's a lot better today, but—"

"I'll deal with it, Mother," Alice interrupted. She glanced at Latimer. "If I come down to the garages in half an hour, Mr. Latimer, perhaps you'd show me what's wrong."

"Certainly, Miss Hurley."

Tom Latimer gave a small, stiff bow and left the two women. His feelings were mixed. He didn't regret the impulse that had made him seek out Alice to discover if she were really ill, but once assured she was all right he might have preferred to leave it at that. He wasn't sure he wanted an assignation with her. It would only mean questions, explanations, lies—or the devastating truth. Silently he cursed the dead Roy Mortlake, and the police.

He met the police, in the persons of Superintendent Thorne and Sergeant Abbot in the hall. They had just arrived and were talking to John Kempton. He tried to slip past them, but Thorne stopped him.

"So you've returned, Latimer?" Thorne pretended surprise. "Good. We'd like a little chat with you. Sergeant Abbot will take you along to our interview room."

"Do you mean right away? I'm busy—er—sir."

"I mean right away." The Superintendent ignored Latimer's rudeness and nodded to Sergeant Abbot before returning his attention to John Kempton. "You were saying—everyone's much better today. At least that's a blessing."

"Indeed it is. A great relief. Some of them feel a bit shaky, but they're all what you might call walking wounded. Even Mrs. Blair's been pottering around her room. She's back to form, according to the maid, complaining furiously. Why hadn't Band been to see her? Where was he?" Kempton shook his head. "Maybe I'd better warn him when he comes, though of course he knows the lady well enough by now."

Thorne grinned. "Any idea what caused the upset yet?"

"None. The health people have been and gone. They inspected the kitchens, but Felix really does keep them spotless. 'As good as any he'd ever seen,' one of the chaps said. They took away a lot more samples, but as far as I

can make out they don't expect them to show anything.
The trouble is the poisoning was so completely random;
there was no pattern at all to it. But it couldn't have
happened at a worse moment from our point of view.
You've heard the radio, seen the papers."

"Yes." Thorne nodded.

"Your men are being very good keeping reporters
away, but what these media chaps can't find out they
bloody well invent." Kempton was bitter. "I'm afraid this
business—on top of the murder—has about done for
Wychwood House."

Thorne said gently, "How's Rose, John?"

"Bearing up. We all are. We had a long talk last
night, the two of us and Paul. Whatever happens we stick
together." Kempton's jaw jutted with determination. "That
shit Mortlake's dead now, and we'll be all right. As soon as
we can Rose and I'll get married and legalize our position.
For the rest, what's done is done. It's the future that
matters, and we'll have to play that by ear. All this is
assuming you don't start running us in for bigamy—or
murder." John Kempton stared at Thorne.

The Superintendent was saved from having to respond by the appearance of Helen Dearden through the
front door. For once she looked somewhat less than her
crisp, efficient self, but she smiled a greeting to both men
before turning to Kempton.

"I'm sorry I'm late, John. I forgot to set my alarm and
I overslept."

"That's okay, Helen, providing nothing's wrong."

"No. Nothing's wrong. I'm fine now. I had a bit of a
billious attack yesterday—too bad having to spend my day
off in bed—but it's cleared up."

Thorne and Kempton exchanged glances. Kempton
was frowning. Helen Dearden looked at them inquiringly.

"Have I said something odd?" she asked.

Thorne answered her. "Mrs. Dearden, some of the
hotel guests suffered from food poisoning on Monday night,
probably as a result of something they ate at Mr. and Mrs.
Fowler's party that evening. Naturally we're wondering—"

"But Helen didn't go to the Fowlers' reception,"

Kempton pointed out. "Nor did she have dinner here afterwards."

"Someone had to be on duty, Superintendent," Helen Dearden said, "and I volunteered. I rarely touch alcohol, and I didn't mind missing the party."

"So you had none of the food—at either the party, or the dinner?" Thorne persisted.

"No. Except for a bit of the big pastry heart that Felix made specially instead of a cake . . ." She stopped as she realized the implication of her words. "Rose brought me a piece, with a glass of champagne," she explained. "She said everyone was having some, and I mustn't be left out. Are—are many of the guests ill?"

"No, not very many, fortunately," Thorne said.

"If only a few were sick it can't have been due to the heart, can it?" Helen Dearden had a logical mind. "Mine must have been an ordinary tummy upset."

"Yes, that would explain it," Thorne agreed readily. He had no wish to pursue the question of Felix's pastry heart, no wish to start rumours before he could make more inquiries. "Anyway, everyone's improving, so there's nothing to be gained by worrying about it. I must be off; I've other business to attend to, don't forget. I'll see you later, John."

Thorne left them hurriedly. He found Abbot outside the interview room talking to the constable on duty there, and drew him aside. "Sergeant Abbot," he said, "a point's just come up. Now, listen . . ." He kept his voice low as he gave his instructions. "And be tactful," he concluded.

"Will do, sir." Bill Abbot grinned. "Latimer's getting impatient," he added, nodding towards the door. "He's twice come out to ask where you were."

"Damned cheek!" the Superintendent said, and went into the room.

Superintendent Thorne's interview with Tom Latimer was protracted and bitter. Thorne came to the point at once; Latimer's fingerprints had been lifted from the glass ashtray he had picked up, and his criminal past was known.

"Criminal past!" Latimer said sarcastically. "You sound like a woman's magazine, Superintendent. Sure, I killed a man. You must know the details. It wasn't intentional, and

I was found guilty of manslaughter. But I got a damned hanging judge, and he gave me six years in one of your filthy overcrowded gaols. As the phrase goes, I've paid. I'll say I've paid! So why should I be suspect number one for Mortlake's murder now?"

"No one said you were, Latimer."

"*Mister* Latimer, Superintendent."

"That's not your real name."

"It's not against the law to use any name you like. My family—especially my distinguished brother—have chosen to disown me. Damn it all, it's catching; now I sound like some wretched magazine! Anyway, I choose not to use my family's name. It's as simple as that."

Thorne changed the subject. "Mr. Kempton doesn't know you're an ex-con. If he were told, do you think he'd continue to employ you?"

"Are you proposing to tell him, Superintendent?"

"That's not the point. The question is—did Roy Mortlake threaten to tell him?"

"Mortlake? Ah, I see—my motive." Latimer laughed. "You're straining for it, Superintendent. I'm no blackmail subject. I'd be sorry to lose this job; I quite enjoy it, and I like the Kemptons. But it wouldn't be the end of the world if I got the sack. I've got a little money, enough for my needs—but not enough to support a blackmailer. No, no. It wouldn't be me he'd have tried to put the black on."

"And just what do you mean by that?" Thorne asked sharply, thinking of the Kemptons.

But Latimer said, "Surely my brother would be a more likely bet."

"Perhaps you wanted to spare your family from having the old disgrace raked up," Thorne said, but even as he spoke he knew it was a weak remark.

So did Tom Latimer, for he didn't bother to reply. Instead he deliberately consulted his watch. "If that's all, Superintendent, *I*'ve got work to do."

"It's not all. Why did you go to London yesterday?"

"To see my lawyer, on private business."

Thorne didn't press. He controlled his irritation and leant back in his chair, regarding Thomas Edward Lane-Coln with a benevolence he didn't feel.

"Let's go over it again," Thorne said. "Do you still maintain you didn't go into the shrubbery on the morning of Mortlake's murder?"

"Yes. I was only at the far edge—the edge away from the swimming pool. I was inspecting a big rhododendron branch that had been damaged by the storm. I told you that before."

"And that was where you were when you saw the Ravens and Canon Hurley?"

"Yes. The Ravens were some distance away across the grass, jogging. The Canon was trudging along, head down, lost in thought. He suddenly turned round and came in my direction. I think he went along the path into the shrubbery but I couldn't swear to it. I wasn't watching. I wasn't particularly interested."

This was the most cooperative answer Latimer had produced, though his main interest, thought Thorne, was probably to be shot of further questioning. He was sitting on the edge of his chair and seemed about to leap to his feet and depart. Thorne stroked his moustache, purposely procrastinating.

Finally he said, "When you heard me talking to Paul Kempton about a bottle of lime juice, you immediately associated it with Mortlake's death. Why?" He waited for Latimer to deny it.

"Why? It's obvious, isn't it? I'd seen the back of Mortlake's head. A so-called blunt instrument would fill the bill. You were interested in a bottle of lime juice. I just put two and two together."

"Okay," Thorne said. "That'll be all for now—Mr. Latimer."

"Thanks."

If Thorne's abrupt dismissal startled Latimer, he gave no sign of it.

For several minutes after Latimer's departure Thorne sat at his desk. He didn't much like the man, he admitted to himself, but almost against his will he believed him, just as he tended to believe the Kemptons. At least the trip to London hadn't been an entirely wasted day, he thought, if only because it had sorted out the backgrounds of these three. Major Winston, however, seemed to have galloped into the distance. The Met's inquiries had found no trace of him at either his club or his house. For the present he was just another loose end, though the search was continuing; the Superintendent wondered whether he should face another encounter with Lady Georgina, but decided to postpone it until some new evidence turned up.

In search of fresh air and fresh ideas, Thorne decided to revisit the scene of the crime. He first walked around the perimeter of the shrubbery. There, on the edge furthest from the swimming pool, just as Tom Latimer had described it, he found a broken rhododendron bush. The bush was in fact acting as one of the supports for the red police tape, which was still *in situ* surrounding the whole area.

From this location, Thorne accepted, Latimer could have seen Canon Hurley—or anyone else—entering the shrubbery path. But the Ravens hadn't seen him, and the Canon himself, though nervous, had vigorously denied being anywhere in the vicinity at the relevant time. Either Latimer or Hurley had lied and, after his recent interview, Thorne had a feeling in his bones that it wasn't Latimer. But why on earth should the Canon have told an untruth—and about such an obviously important detail? There had been no suggestion whatsoever of any connection between him and Roy Mortlake.

Shaking his head, the Superintendent ducked under the police tape and set off down the path, following the way the murdered man had presumably taken the previous Friday. He stopped by the spot, still carefully covered by tarpaulins, where the killing had almost certainly taken place, but no inspiration came and he went on to the swimming pool. A fruitless effort, he thought as, again avoiding the tape, he passed gloomily through the stone archway. It was here that Sergeant Abbot hailed him.

"Sir! I've been looking for you."

"Well, here I am, if you've any momentous news, Sergeant."

"Scarcely that, sir, but I've inquired about that pastry heart, as you suggested. The Frenchman made it himself, with some kind of special filling—savoury, it was supposed to be. He wouldn't let anyone else touch it, according to the kitchen maid I talked to." Abbot couldn't resist the temptation to pause dramatically. "But it was put out on the table in the party room a good half-hour before the guests arrived! Felix arranged it himself."

"Half an hour?" said Thorne thoughtfully. "Plenty of time for someone to pop into the room and tamper with it. So did anyone? Have we had any report on those food samples?"

"No luck, sir. The damned heart was completely finished at the party. All the cooking utensils were washed up beforehand, and even the dish it was on has gone through the washer by now."

"Damn!" said Thorne. "Just our luck!"

"Anyway, sir, everyone wasn't sick, so only a part of the thing could have been poisoned. There wasn't a chance of attacking any particular individual that way, was there?"

"I've no idea, Sergeant Abbot. Your guess is as good as mine—"

"Sir?" Abbot questioned as Thorne suddenly stopped speaking.

The Superintendent didn't answer at once. He was staring up at the house, at the corner windows on the first floor. Then he turned and glanced back at the archway through which he had just passed.

"That room up there," he said at last, pointing. "Shouldn't that be Cassandra Gray's?"

Abbot oriented himself. "Yes, sir. I think so. Why?"

"There was an article on her in the *Sunday Times* colour magazine last weekend," Thorne said. Miranda had read parts of it to him, but he'd paid little attention; he'd been too busy wondering whether to take seriously his Chief's warning against being biased in favour of the Kemptons. But the odd sentence had penetrated. "It said she likes to get up early every morning and sit by a window with a view and write," he remarked. "Let's go and ask her about last Friday."

The two detectives found Cassandra Gray in the lounge finishing her coffee and buttered toast. Her mind was still on her work, and she wasn't altogether pleased to see them. Her previous interview with Superintendent Thorne had been fairly cursory. She had answered the questions he asked, but volunteered nothing. Now he was more persistent and, having nothing to hide and wanting to be rid of them, she replied freely.

"Yes," she said, "I was sitting at my desk on Friday morning, working, but glancing up from time to time. It's my habit. Whom did I see? You mean, before Mrs. Raven came running. I saw her, though of course I didn't know then what it was all about. Before that—only Canon Hurley."

Miss Gray was vague about exact times, but certain of her facts. She had seen Canon Hurley hurry through the archway from the swimming pool fifteen minutes or so before Mrs. Raven had given the alarm.

They tackled the Canon next. He was still in his room, wearing pyjamas and a handsome purple dressing-gown. Confronted with the new evidence about his movements, his responses became minimal and stilted. Whatever he'd said before, he didn't really remember. He certainly didn't think he'd gone through the shrubbery that morning, but he supposed he might have. He'd had a lot on his mind. But none of it concerned Mr. Mortlake, and he knew nothing about him or his death.

With that they had to be content. For the moment, Thorne thought to himself as he concluded the unsatisfactory interview.

# Chapter 14

At least two of the inhabitants of Wychwood House were to be pleased that Thursday.

When Alice Hurley woke she noticed an envelope lying on the floor just inside her door. She assumed it was some announcement concerning the hotel, and she made no immediate attempt to retrieve it. She lay in bed, hands behind her head, and thought about Tom Latimer.

They were not happy thoughts. Yesterday morning she had waited for what seemed like hours by the garages, but he hadn't arrived. Disappointed in spite of herself, she had rationalized her feelings: she was a fool, she should have more pride, her father was right and the sooner he got his way and they all left Wychwood House the better; they would never see the place again, and she was glad; altogether it had been a disastrous holiday.

At last, languidly, she got out of bed and went to pick up the envelope. It was clearly no hotel circular, for it was addressed to her in unfamiliar handwriting, and marked "Personal." Her interest aroused, she tore it open and turned to the signature at the end of what was clearly a long letter. She had never heard the name Thomas Lane-Coln, but she knew at once that the letter was from Tom Latimer. She read:

Dear Alice,
    Whatever you may feel about me, please, please read this right through to the end and then try to understand, to put yourself in my place.

117

I couldn't meet you yesterday morning because I was being grilled by Superintendent Thorne about Mortlake's murder. I know nothing about it, but Thorne has discovered that I'm an ex-convict. I killed a man when I found he was sleeping with my girlfriend. It was at a party. I hit him and he went over the edge of a balcony. A couple of his friends said I could easily have saved him if I'd wanted to, and honestly I don't know. Like everyone else I was a bit drunk. Anyway, the judge took a dim view and I spent six years in prison, which was hell.

Afterwards my family preferred not to know me. I took my godmother's name—Latimer—drifted around and finally landed up here, at Wychwood House. So much for my life story. I'm not what could be called a desirable character. I'm sure your father would never approve of me. However . . .

It's hard to know how to put this—except bluntly. I began by feeling a little sorry for you, and grew to like you, more and more. Now I believe I'm in love with you. I'm no catch. That's obvious. But such as I am, if you want me I'm yours. Will you marry me? Please think about it very carefully before you decide.

Clutching the letter, Alice got back into bed. She was crying and smiling at the same time. She read the letter again. She had no need to think carefully. She knew. They would wait till this horrible business of Roy Mortlake was over and done with. Then, whatever her father might say . . .

Though Lady Georgina Winston had quite recovered from her poisoning, she had breakfasted in her room, and hadn't yet bothered to dress when there was a loud banging on the door of her suite. Grabbing a robe and prepared to be indignant, she went to open it.

"Derek?"

Georgina Winston stared at her husband in disbelief.

He was wearing jeans, a fisherman's jersey and rubber Wellington boots. He looked tired and not too clean, and there was a three-day growth of beard on his face. But she had never before been so glad to see him.

"Darling, where have you been?" she cried as he came into the room. "I've been trying to find you everywhere. The police want to talk to you and I didn't know what to say. I've been so worried."

"Damn the police! What about you? Are you all right, Georgie? You don't look well. To think I left you alone in a place with a madman at large. Will you ever forgive me?"

They spoke at the same time, each scarcely listening to the other, but it didn't matter. They were overjoyed that they were both well and safe. Explanations could wait, Derek Winston said, and picking up his wife with some difficulty, he carried her into the bedroom.

A while later a happy and relaxed Lady Georgina declared that they really must telephone the police and explain what had happened. They discussed the details for a little while and then the Major got through to Thorne. He immediately launched into an account of his movements, but the Superintendent cut him short. Thorne said he would be at Wychwood House within the next hour, and would be grateful if both Major Winston and his wife were there waiting for him.

Derek Winston put down the receiver and grimaced. "That Superintendent doesn't sound too friendly," he said. "I've a nasty feeling this meeting's going to be sticky—something like a court martial, say."

In the event, Superintendent Thorne greeted the Winstons with the utmost courtesy, waving them to chairs and asking the Major to tell his story at his convenience and in his own words. Only Sergeant Abbot, sitting unobtrusively with his notebook to one side of the room, appreciated that Thorne's affability was deceptive. The police had spent a lot of time and effort trying to trace this man, who'd now turned up out of the blue, apparently unabashed.

"It's really very simple, Superintendent," Major Winston said, smiling pleasantly if a shade patronizingly. "I got up at crack of dawn last Friday and drove up to

London. I met a chum, did a spot of business with him, but failed to get hold of someone else I wanted. Now, I'd told Georgie here that I'd be away for a couple of days, so when my chum told me he was taking his boat over to France for the weekend and asked me to crew for him, I agreed. It wasn't till I saw an English paper yesterday that I knew about all the mayhem that had been going on in this place. Of course I dashed back as fast as I could to make sure Georgie was okay."

Leaning towards his wife Major Winston patted her affectionately on the thigh. In return she seized his hand and squeezed it. Their apparent devotion to each other hardly jibed with what Thorne had already heard about them.

Lady Georgina smoothed her skirt over her knees. "So I hope that's satisfactory, Superintendent," she said, "because we're thinking of leaving Wychwood House later today. A quick visit to our boys over at Coriston, and then back to London."

"I can't imagine why it should be necessary," the Major added, "but you can always contact us there. You must have the address."

"Your address? Indeed yes, sir," Thorne said. "But not the address of that chum you speak of."

"No—er, but why . . ." Major Winston stared truculently at the Superintendent. "Surely you can't doubt—"

"All statements have to be verified, sir." Thorne was at his blandest. "What time did you leave the hotel on Friday morning?"

Winston shrugged. "Soon after six. The night porter will verify *that*," he remarked sarcastically. "I wanted to avoid the traffic. I went straight to my car and drove off. I saw no one else."

"And Lady Georgina knew where you'd gone?"

"I told you, Superintendent!" Lady Georgina was indignant. "I wasn't sure where my husband was staying, but I knew he was in London on business."

"Yes, that's what you told me," Thorne agreed. "But wouldn't it have been nearer the truth if you'd admitted you'd no idea of his whereabouts?"

"Certainly not! I resent that suggestion."

"Then why did you spend so much time on the phone on Friday trying to locate him?"

It was a guess on Thorne's part. The hotel's automatic system clocked up Lady Georgina's many calls, but there was no record of whom she had phoned, let alone why. But the guess paid off. Lady Georgina stammered a denial, blustered, then told Thorne it was none of his business whom she'd telephoned.

"Everything concerned with a murder inquiry is my business," the Superintendent said portentously. "So let's start again, and this time perhaps you'll be more—more accurate, shall we say? On Thursday evening last you and Major Winston quarrelled over Roy Mortlake . . ."

Pretending to know more than you did was an age-old ploy, George Thorne thought, but it worked. It was still one of the best ways of extracting information from reluctant witnesses. Now he listened with satisfaction as the Winstons talked.

They admitted to their quarrel, though they brushed off the reason for it as irrelevant. Mortlake was totally unimportant, they said. Unfortunately they were inclined to quarrel over pointless things. Thursday night's incident had arisen because the Major had been admiring the young American girl's figure at the swimming pool. During dinner he'd accused his wife of making a pass at Roy Mortlake to get her revenge, and the argument had exploded.

Anyway, that night the Major had slept on the sofa in the sitting-room of their suite, and early in the morning had departed without telling his wife, not to London, but to a south coast town where a friend kept a boat. Until yesterday, as he'd already stated, he'd been in France, and he could prove this if necessary. He'd returned as soon as he saw an English newspaper. Georgina—well, Georgina had been out of her mind with worry. He was sorry for distressing her, and for any trouble he'd caused the police. The whole thing had been stupid and unnecessary.

Thorne was inclined to believe them, though he pressed them about the cause of their quarrel. They maintained it was unimportant.

"So utterly silly," Lady Georgina said.

"But regrettable," Thorne said, "seeing that a few hours later Mortlake lost the back of his skull."

The Winstons were silent. Nor did they protest when Thorne said he wished them to remain at Wychwood House for the present. They departed, their manner a good deal less assured than when they had arrived.

As soon as they had gone, Thorne sent Sergeant Abbot to ask William Fowler to spare him a few minutes. The lawyer, however, could only reiterate what he had said before. He had overheard very little of the Winstons' conversation, though, yes, he had been struck by the intensity of feeling they seemed to be generating.

Thorne thanked him and Fowler half rose from his chair, but sat back again, looking slightly embarrassed. "Superintendent," he said, "I wouldn't like you to think I make a habit of eavesdropping, but my conscience has been troubling me a little—" He paused.

"This *is* a murder case, sir." Thorne did his best to sound sympathetic, and wondered what was to come.

"I know." Fowler sighed. "Well, after I heard the Winstons arguing I went upstairs and . . ."

The lawyer described the acrimonious conversation in the doorway of Mortlake's room between the murdered man and John Kempton. "I did mention it to Kempton," he added, "and he said he'd been asking Mortlake to leave the hotel because of the unpleasantness with Paul, and the man had turned nasty. His explanation was reasonable enough, except—"

"Except what, sir?"

"Well, I never told Kempton I'd heard the word 'rosebud'—somehow it seemed very private—nor did I mention the threat Kempton made."

"You're sure about that, sir—sure of the words, I mean? Mr. Kempton said, 'If you do anything to hurt her, I'll kill you.' "

William Fowler sighed again. "Yes, Superintendent, I'm sure."

"And he calls himself a lawyer," Abbot said with disgust when Fowler had been dismissed. "Withholding evidence, that's what it was. Of all the people at Wychwood

House, he should have known better. Don't you agree, sir?"

"Yes," said Thorne. He was thinking sadly that the case against John Kempton was now as strong as could be expected, barring a confession. Sure, the DPP might settle for a charge of manslaughter, and the evidence was secondary and circumstantial so that a clever defending barrister might win a minimal sentence for his client, but still . . .

During the afternoon Canon Hurley complained of feeling less well. He hoped he wasn't getting hepatitis again; he'd had a couple of previous attacks and his liver function tests had never been completely normal. But the signs were unmistakable. His urine was a dark amber colour, and the whites of his eyes were turning yellow. Perhaps, he suggested tentatively, they should send for Dr. Band.

Margaret Hurley hid her surprise at this request. The Canon wasn't apt to be so eager for medical advice; usually she had to persuade him to seek it. She phoned Dr. Band's surgery, to be told the doctor was on his rounds, but the message would reach him as soon as possible. She refused the services of Band's partner. Her husband wouldn't want to be attended by a stranger if it could be avoided. They would wait for Dr. Band.

Alice agreed. There was no need for over-anxiety. If her mother had no objection she would get a little fresh air. When her mother suggested that she should not go far from the hotel, Alice willingly acquiesced and promised not to be long. All she wanted was an opportunity to speak to Tom Latimer.

She found Latimer sawing logs, and stacking them in a garden shed to dry out. She had expected their meeting to be embarrassing, but it wasn't.

"I told you to think carefully before deciding," he said, grinning at her.

"I know, but it wasn't necessary. The answer's yes. I love you, Tom. I want to marry you."

"In spite of all the problems?"

"Yes. We'll—we'll cope with them together."

The first—and probably the worst, Alice thought, would be telling her father. She decided to do this at once, in spite of his illness. But she was frustrated. By the time she got back to her parents' room Dr. Band had arrived and arrangements were being made to take the Canon, whose condition had deteriorated, by ambulance to Oxford.

"What is it, doctor? Hepatitis again?" she asked.

"To be honest, I'm not sure, Miss Hurley," Band admitted. "Certainly your father has some of the signs and symptoms, but . . . Anyway, the first thing is to get him into hospital where they can do all the tests and give him proper attention."

"He looks dreadfully ill, doctor," Margaret Hurley said anxiously. "You don't think it could be connected with the food poisoning he's had, do you?"

Band merely said, "It's no use guessing, Mrs. Hurley. We'll have to wait. Try not to worry."

They had been standing by the window, talking softly, backs half turned to the bed where Canon Hurley lay. The sick man appeared to be asleep. But suddenly he spoke.

"It's God's vengeance," he said. "He has smitten me, and I'm about to die."

"No, no, Peter, you'll be all right soon." Margaret Hurley hurried to the bed and took his hand.

"Yes," the Canon said. "I shall die, as—as a reparation for what I did to Roy Mortlake."

# Chapter 15

"So it was a kind of death-bed confession?" Superintendent Thorne shook his head doubtfully.

"I suppose you could call it that," said Band, "though the man's not dead—yet."

"I know," said Thorne. "God! I wish I could talk to him."

"There's no chance of that, not for a while—if ever."

It was late in the evening. The two men sat in a consultant's office at the Radcliffe Infirmary in Oxford. Canon Hurley was in an intensive care unit, his wife and daughter in a room nearby where they could be sent for in case of need.

George Thorne pulled at his moustache, and listened to the muted sounds of hospital life outside the office door. He was considering what Dr. Band had told him, and how much of it he should believe. Not for a moment did he doubt Dick Band's account, but the story told by the Canon was a different matter.

According to Band, the Canon had been insistent that the doctor, rather than his family, should travel with him in the ambulance to Oxford. He had murmured incoherently that he was convinced he was going to die, and must clear his conscience by telling someone in authority, and Band had acquiesced.

In the ambulance he had seemed to recover somewhat, and what he had to "confess" was quite clear. Last Friday morning the Canon had been unable to sleep because of his wife's constant coughing. He had risen early,

contrary to his habit when on holiday, and gone for a walk
in the grounds of Wychwood House. By chance he had
come across Roy Mortlake. He had no particular liking for
the man but was about to make a polite remark when, to
his surprise and subsequent consternation, Mortlake had
greeted him with hilarity and asked if he was in search of
his daughter. To use Mortlake's expression, Alice was
busy "having it off" with Latimer, the odd job man.

Leaving the Canon speechless with anger at such a
suggestion, Mortlake had departed in the direction of the
shrubbery and its path. The Canon had followed after
some minutes—it was, after all, the shortest way back to
the hotel—and had found Mortlake lying beside the path
with his skull crushed. He had been sure Mortlake was
dead and his first reaction had been thankfulness that the
man could never spread any more of his filthy rumours
about Alice, or anyone else. Then—it must have been a
trick of the light falling through the overhead canopy of
leaves, but at the time he took it for reality—Mortlake's
face suddenly seemed to leer at him.

And without warning the Canon was possessed by
madness. Before he knew what he was doing he had
seized Mortlake under the armpits, dragged him the short
distance to the pool and pushed him in. God help him! In
intention, if not in deed, he had murdered Roy Mortlake.

The story rang true, Thorne concluded; it fitted the
known facts, and from what he knew of Canon Hurley—
and Latimer and even Hurley's daughter—it was not out
of character. But the story was of little help towards solving the crime. It couldn't even reasonably be said to
exonerate the Canon himself. Maybe Hurley had smashed
in Mortlake's head, but couldn't bring himself to accept
his total guilt. It wouldn't be the first time such a partial
"confession" had been made by the guilty; people's minds
worked in funny ways when they were under stress.

Band had been resting his head in his hands, deep in
thought. "Surely no one could be so evil," he said suddenly and unexpectedly.

"What?"

"Sorry. I was thinking aloud. Let's accept Canon Hurley's tale. But suppose he saw or heard something that

would point the finger at Mortlake's murderer—or the murderer thought he did. Then the killer might have planned to get rid of him. Fair enough, but surely he wouldn't have been prepared to cause the death of heaven knows how many irrelevant people."

The Superintendent looked at Band oddly. "Dick, you're talking in riddles. You said Hurley had a weakness in his liver or a history of liver disease. So why should his present condition be connected with the food poisoning scare at the hotel?"

"I'm not sure." Band got up and began to pace the room. "But now we know the Canon *was* involved with Mortlake's murder, even if only after the event, and—and I'm—scared."

"What of?" Thorne was impatient. "Even if some of that pastry heart was deliberately poisoned there was no guarantee the Canon—or anyone else—would eat any particular bit. We've been over all this before."

"Supposing someone made sure he got a poisoned portion by passing it to him. That someone would have been prepared to take the risk that others—many others—would die too. That's what I meant about evil."

"But no one else *is* ill, and it's four days since they ate that damned bit of pastry."

"I know. That's one encouraging point: that the Canon's relapse—assuming it is a relapse—has occurred so soon. But on the other hand he had this history of liver weakness to start with, which might account for—"

"Dick, for God's sake! What are you talking about?"

"Sorry," said Band again. "Put it down to worry. I was forgetting you weren't here when I talked to the consultant. But it's only an idea. Though not a happy one, George."

"Tell me."

Before Band could reply the door was flung open and the consultant who owned the office came in. Dr. Crewe was a man in his forties, tall, gangling, red-haired, blue-eyed. He stared at Thorne and was introduced.

"Bad news, gentlemen," he said. "Canon Hurley died a few minutes ago. Cause of death, liver and kidney failure, as far as I can make out." He glanced at Band. "You could be right, doctor, let's hope you're not. We'll know more after the PM, with luck. What made you think of it?"

"I had a case about a year ago. The stuff does grow in the neighbourhood, and it's easy to mistake for the ordinary field variety."

Thorne was about to open his mouth when Band went on. "What about the others in the meantime, until we're sure?" he asked.

"I know. It's a problem. Wait for the PM results? That might make things worse. Really, we ought to bring them all in for observation, but we don't want to do that unnecessarily. Anyway, having waited so long, there's not much we could do for them."

Thorne had never seen Band so obviously moved. "God!" said the doctor. "That young American on his honeymoon. The Blairs. Lady Georgina. They were affected most acutely, so presumably they're the most unlikely . . ." He couldn't bring himself to finish.

Superintendent Thorne could contain himself no longer. "Will someone please tell me what all this is about?" he demanded. "Have we got an epidemic of some kind, or—"

Crewe unlocked a cabinet and produced a bottle of whisky and three glasses. "I think we could all do with a drink first."

It was an excellent malt, but Thorne was in no mood to appreciate it. After a couple of sips he put down his glass and said firmly, "Now, let's get to the point."

Crewe nodded. "Yes, Superintendent, but remember that what I've got to say is only a possibility." He paused, then continued slowly. "Canon Hurley may have died as the direct result of poison ingested at Wychwood House last Monday. If Dr. Band here is right in thinking that the poison in question was *Amanita phalloides*, then anyone else who had a similar amount—it doesn't have to be much—is also likely to die."

"*Amanita phalloides?*"

"Better known as 'Death Cap.' It's the most deadly fungus—mushroom—there is. And it's particularly nasty because it's so difficult to diagnose. It's like this. The preliminary syndrome—vomiting, diarrhœa, abdominal pain—is similar to that of ordinary food poisoning, or even a common bacterial gastro-enteritis. There's no known antidote to phalloidine poisoning, but if it's diagnosed at that stage it can be treated—gastric lavage, general supportive treatment, that sort of thing.

"The trouble with phalloidine is the diagnosis," Crewe went on. "After about a day the patient appears to recover, so most cases remain undiagnosed and untreated. In fact, the poison's still attacking the liver and the kidneys, and in a few days—usually five to eight—from the onset, the patient becomes ill again. And by this time there's very little hope."

Thorne had no need to hear more; he had grasped the significance of the consultant's words and was appalled. As Crewe reiterated that he was speaking only of a possibility, the Superintendent sought grounds for hope.

"The Canon never ate mushrooms," he said. "They disagreed with him and he always took care to avoid them. What's more, we're as certain as we can be that the source of the poison was that wretched pastry heart."

Even as he spoke Thorne realized the fallacy in his argument. Someone—presumably Roy Mortlake's murderer—could have ground up the fungus and added it before the party to the soft, absorbent savoury filling of the heart-shaped pastry shell.

All the same it didn't make sense. If the murderer was scared that Hurley might know too much, why had he waited till Monday before attempting to dispose of him, thus giving him plenty of time to disclose whatever he knew—and why choose such a bizarre and uncertain method? Thorne swore softly to himself.

"So what do we do now?" he asked.

"Not much," said the doctors simultaneously.

Then Crewe added, "Primarily, keep a strict eye on any candidates." He glanced at Band again, who nodded. "I suppose the thing to look for is any sign of jaundice— yellowing eyes, yellowing skin, aversion to food."

"What about—" began Band.

"I know what you're going to suggest, and I agree," said Crewe. "There *is* one simple test for liver involve-

ment you might be able to use without creating panic. If
you can think of a way to get a regular urine sample from
each of the people concerned and check its colour, it
might give some early warning. There'll be precious little
we can do, but at least you'll know."

"Do we wait for the PM, or not?" Band asked.

Crewe looked at Thorne. "I'd say that was up to the
Superintendent. Personally I'd recommend waiting on the
grounds that there's damn all to be lost, medically speaking, and there's no point in terrifying people over what's
just a possibility."

Thorne shook his head in disagreement. "We need to
know," he said. "With Dr. Band's help we can invent some
fictitious reason for getting samples."

To say there was panic next morning at Wychwood
House would be an exaggeration, but an air of nervous
apprehension certainly pervaded the hotel.

The news of Canon Hurley's death during the night
had spread as soon as Mrs. Hurley and Alice returned from
Oxford, and it was unfortunate that their appearance was
almost immediately followed by the arrival of Dr. Band
with a supply of stoppered test tubes and a request for
urine samples immediately, and each morning for the next
few days. His assurances that this was just a routine check
required by the health authorities after the outbreak of
food poisoning earlier in the week were believed by no
one. But all agreed to return to their rooms and await his
rounds, as it were.

"You must tell us the truth, doctor," Mrs. Blair insisted
when he reached her. "Is there some epidemic? One
reads such dreadful stories about how diseases can be
transmitted, just by shaking hands or something like that."

Dick Band, who had spent a troubled, sleepless night,
was tempted to tell her the truth. Instead, he did his best
to quiet her fears. Maurice Blair, he thought, was being
an unconscionable time in the bathroom.

"There you are," Blair said, emerging. "Sorry to be so
long, but nowadays the old bladder won't always deliver
when asked. Age, I suppose."

"Thanks," Band said and went into the bathroom, shutting the door behind him.

He was only interested in urine that was dark and discoloured. So far he had found none. Even the samples provided by Vern Raven and Lady Georgina, who had previously shown the most acute symptoms of poisoning, were normal. Enormously relieved, he had begun to think that his suspicions were idiotic and that Canon Hurley's death was unrelated to the earlier outbreak.

One glance at the two neatly-labelled test tubes beside the wash basin was enough to shatter this fond hope. Nina Blair's urine was a deep orangey-brown shade, Maurice's much paler but still with a definite yellow tinge. Band stared at them helplessly. All his worst fears had been confirmed. He was surprised he had noticed no change in Mrs. Blair's complexion, but he had had no chance to examine her eyes.

Another ambulance, and the departure of the Blairs to hospital, was the last straw for the guests who remained at Wychwood House. The Fowlers discussed going to stay with their friends, the Railtons. The Ravens considered calling the American ambassador, who was a chum of Vern's father and would surely get someone to advise them. The Winstons announced that they were leaving, police or no police. Cassandra Gray, unable to concentrate on her work, quietly began to pack. And the Kemptons wondered whether they should close the hotel—assuming that Superintendent Thorne would allow them to do so.

In spite of this confusion, the situation had improved slightly by the time Thorne and Abbot reached Wychwood House. Advised by phone about the Blairs, the Superintendent had feared the worst, and was relieved to learn from Dr. Band that no one else on the premises appeared to be in danger at the moment. What was more, the reports that had come in on the health of all the others who had been guests at the party showed that none had suffered any ill-effects.

"Which means—apart from Mortlake himself—we've got one dead and two others likely to die," the Superintendent said to Abbot. "It's not enough, you know, Sergeant."

Abbot stared at him. "Not enough? I'd have thought it was more than—" he began, and stopped himself from saying something he might later regret. "I don't understand, sir," he amended hurriedly.

"According to the medics you don't need much of the *Amanita phalloides* to do for you. It's not called 'Death Cap' for nothing. Now, everyone at the Fowlers' party, plus Mrs. Dearden, had a bit of that pastry heart, but not all of them were ill. Therefore, only a part of the thing was poisoned. Fair enough. But . . ." Thorne paused. He had been thinking aloud. Now he turned to Abbot triumphantly. "A lot of them were ill—several very ill—to start with. Sergeant Abbot, I've briefed you on these curious delayed effects of poisoning by this damned mushroom. Why are so few of these people—just three, to be exact, and not even all those who were worst hit before—in any danger now?"

Abbot had followed the Superintendent's line of reasoning, but he could think of no sensible answer to the final question. "I really have no idea, sir," he admitted.

"Just suppose, Sergeant Abbot, that there were two poisons. Something comparatively innocuous in the pastry heart, so that quite a few of the guests would have symptoms of ordinary food poisoning. Then the really deadly stuff, administered to Canon Hurley and the Blairs."

"But how, sir? And there's still the question of 'why.' "

"As to 'how,' I don't know—yet," Thorne said grimly. "I intend to find out. The 'why' is simple. To throw us off the scent by confusing the issues, and preventing wretched Dr. Band from making a correct diagnosis."

"But I mean why those three, sir? The Canon seems to have got himself involved with Mortlake's death, but how do the Blairs fit in?"

"Again, I don't know," Thorne admitted, "but I've a feeling that if we could discover how they were poisoned, the 'why' might answer itself. At any rate, I think we're pointed in the right direction at last."

"It's going to mean a lot of digging, sir," Sergeant Abbot said doubtfully.

"So the sooner we start the better." Thorne was adamant. "What we need is something that Canon Hurley and the Blairs ate, but no one else. Something that could have had this *Amanita phalloides* added to it."

"Yes, sir," Abbot said, and thought that they'd been through all this before, give or take the mushroom bit, and they'd come up with a great round zero. Personally, he couldn't see why they should be any luckier a second time.

# Chapter 16

Saturday morning, and Superintendent Thorne was thinking how pleasant it would be if his was one of those professions where weekends were sacrosanct and meant time to please oneself, to do whatever took one's fancy. For a senior police officer in the middle of a murder case, Saturday merely meant another hard day of work—and he hoped more profitable work than he had managed yesterday. For yesterday had seen no progress at all with the inquiry.

He grunted his thanks as his wife placed a plate before him—a fried egg, two rashers of bacon and a fried tomato. Sometimes he had mushrooms for breakfast, but he was glad there were none this morning. He doubted if he would ever again eat mushrooms with pleasure.

Miranda, who sat opposite him at the kitchen table, put down her cup as she heard the clatter of the daily newspapers being pushed through the letter-box. She got up and went to fetch them.

The Thornes took one of the so-called "quality" papers and a tabloid. Returning with them, Miranda said, "Wychwood House has made the front page again in this rag, George. There's a picture of the Blairs."

"Let me see." Thorne held out his hand.

It was a photograph taken some years ago, but the Blairs were recognizable at a glance; Maurice's stiff-backed stance and Nina's pretty, petulant face were unmistakable. The caption below gave their names, and referred to them as two more victims of the "Hotel of Horror." The story—a couple of paragraphs beside the picture—was noticeably weak on factual information. It merely reported that the Blairs had been taken to hospital with suspected poisoning, and coupled this event with the death of Canon Hurley and the killing of Roy Mortlake. Without actually saying so, it managed to imply that all the guests at the Wychwood House Hotel were at risk.

"Poor Kemptons." Miranda read the piece over her husband's shoulder and repeated the comment she had made so many times in the last few days. "It *is* a shame. They've worked so hard to make it a success, and now through no fault of their own . . ."

Thorne said nothing. He passed Miranda the paper and returned to his breakfast. It was ironic, he thought, but if it hadn't been for the death of Canon Hurley from phalloidine poisoning, John Kempton might well by now have been charged with Mortlake's murder. The Chief Constable had considered the case against him adequate to put before the DPP, and he had only hesitated when Thorne pointed out that, as a townsman, Kempton was unlikely to know one fungus from another or to choose such a means of poisoning anyone. But it was a reprieve for Kempton, no more. Unless some fresh evidence turned up pretty rapidly . . .

George Thorne finished the last of his bacon and pushed his cup towards Miranda for more tea. He buttered toast and reached for the marmalade. "The poisoner must have known where to find these wretched Death Caps," he said. "He couldn't have just dreamt up the idea, and gone out and picked a couple. Which means he must be well acquainted with the neighbourhood. Probably he goes for long walks—you'd have to be on foot to find the damned things. I asked Bill Abbot—after all he was brought up in Colombury and supposedly might have been warned against touching them when he was a kid—but he had no idea where they might grow."

"Why don't you ask Cassandra Gray?" Miranda said.

"What?" Thorne slowly put down his cup. Miranda wasn't in the habit of making pointless remarks. "Why Cassandra Gray? What's she got to do with it?"

"Because she's keen on walking—and on wild flowers and nature and things like that."

"How do you know?"

"George, there was that article on her in the *Sunday Times*. I read it to you. Weren't you listening?"

"Not terribly hard," Thorne admitted. "Obviously I should have been. Have we still got it?"

"Yes. I'll fetch it."

Thorne read the article—"A Day in the Life of . . ."—with care. Cassandra Gray gave her hobbies as bird watching, nature study, walking, solving puzzles. "She sounds better equipped than I am to deal with this case," he said wryly.

Miranda produced more toast. "Tea?" she asked, lifting the pot.

"Please," Thorne said. "But first I must make a quick phone call to Wychwood House. Miss Gray was going to leave today. I hope I can catch her."

"Another ten minutes and I'd have gone," Cassandra Gray said when he got through and explained what he wanted. "I've a long drive ahead of me, Superintendent. Is it really necessary I wait for you?"

"Please, yes," Thorne insisted. "If, without mentioning it to anyone, you could meet me . . ."

"Sounds as if you're making an assignation, George," Miranda said as the Superintendent returned to his breakfast. "Successful, I hope?"

"I'll tell you that tonight, my dear," Thorne said, grinning.

A little more than an hour later, Superintendent Thorne picked up Miss Gray at the end of the Wychwood House drive. He sat in the back of the car with her, while Sergeant Abbot drove.

"You understand I can't guarantee there'll be any there now," she said. "But I can take you to a place where I spotted a little group of *Amanita phalloides* about two weeks ago. I noticed them particularly. They've a beautiful pale green sheen on the cap and, of course, they're frightfully deadly. Do you believe—? Or should I not ask questions?"

"We don't know, Miss Gray," Thorne smiled ruefully. "It's a very puzzling case, this."

"You can count on my discretion, Superintendent."

"Yes, Miss Gray. We know that. Otherwise we wouldn't have asked you to help us this morning." Thorne hesitated. Cassandra Gray was an intelligent woman who would already have reached her own conclusions. There might be something to be gained by exchanging confidences. He said, "One possible theory is that whoever killed Mr. Mortlake feared that Canon Hurley—and perhaps Mr. or Mrs. Blair—might have seen—"

Miss Gray interrupted him. "That's not the only possibility, surely, Superintendent, though of course it's the obvious one. I imagine that in most crimes you deal with the obvious solution is the right one in the end, but—"

It was Thorne's turn to interrupt. "Not if the crimes happen in this part of the country," he said grimly.

Behind the wheel, Sergeant Abbot, listening to the conversation, concealed his amusement. He liked Cassandra Gray. She was, he thought, one of the few people they'd come across who was a match for Superintendent Thorne.

"Have you considered the possibility that it might be the other way round, Superintendent?" Miss Gray suggested tentatively. "I expect you have. Personally I think it would make more sense, though naturally I've no idea of any motive."

"The other way round?" Thorne said, surprised. No one, to his knowledge, had considered the theory that Roy Mortlake might have been killed because *he* knew something that would point a finger at the would-be murderer of Canon Hurley or the Blairs. It was certainly an interesting speculation, but . . .

As if to give him a moment to ponder the matter Miss Gray leant forward to speak to Abbot. "Keep right at the next crossroads," she said. "Then right again and, after about a half mile, keep left. You'll be able to get off the road there, and we can walk." She glanced at Thorne's feet. "I hope you've both got stout shoes," she added.

"Yes, madam," Abbot said, slowing as he approached the crossroads.

The Superintendent grunted, knowing perfectly well

that his shoes were totally unsuitable for tramping around the countryside. Then he said, "Miss Gray, I see what you mean, but why should it make more sense?"

"Well," said Miss Gray, "for one thing, it eliminates the need to explain the delay between Mr. Mortlake's death and the Canon's. Look, someone plans to poison the Canon. He knows where to find *Amanita phalloides*, but he's seen picking it by Mr. Mortlake, so poor Mr. Mortlake has to die before the poison can be used."

"It's an interesting idea, Miss Gray," Thorne agreed. His first surprise had passed. He reminded himself that Cassandra Gray knew nothing of the Kemptons' motive for wishing Mortlake out of the way, nor of Canon Hurley's strange "confession." Mortlake hadn't been a pleasant type; on the surface he was a much more likely candidate for murder than the old Canon. "If only there was some evidence to support it," he added.

"Mr. Mortlake used to walk in the woods. He was there the Thursday before he was killed. I saw him myself."

"Indeed!" said Thorne, swallowing hard.

"I'll show you, Superintendent. We're almost there. And if you're thinking we're a long way from Wychwood House, we are—by these local roads. But I'm sure you've noticed we've come round in a kind of circle, and there are paths across the fields that cut the distance considerably."

They had now reached a stretch of straight road with what seemed to be a good-sized wood on one side. Obeying Miss Gray's directions, Sergeant Abbot turned on to a small grassed area, and parked under the trees. Miss Gray was out of the car before he could open the door for her. The Superintendent took his time; he wasn't expecting to enjoy the next half-hour or so.

Cassandra Gray led the way at a brisk pace. It was a day of low cloud, and gloomy in the wood. Some of the trees were already beginning to shed their leaves, which made a slippery mulch underfoot. Several times Thorne nearly fell. But, biting his tongue to prevent himself from swearing aloud, he followed grimly, unhappily aware that Abbot, loping along behind with easy strides, was probably enjoying his ineptitude.

The path, though little more than a track, was clearly defined. It suddenly debouched into a clearing. Miss Gray stopped. At one side was a splendid oak tree. She pointed and moved towards it. "Isn't it magnificent?" she said, patting the bark as if it were an old friend. "This is where the Death Caps were, Superintendent, growing under the oak. They like oaks."

"So I've read," said Thorne. Then, "They *were* here, you said? But no longer?"

"No, Superintendent. There were only two or three, you know, and they've quite disappeared. It's possible someone's picked them."

"Why do you say that?"

"That someone's picked them? Well, I doubt if they'd have decomposed naturally in the time, without leaving any traces."

"Thank you, Miss Gray." One of George Thorne's many saving graces was that he was always prepared to appreciate expertise in others. "Now, let's get the times straight. Exactly when were they here? And are you certain?"

"Yes." There was no hesitation on Miss Gray's part. "I saw them only once, the Monday before last. The day," she added, "that the Hurleys arrived at Wychwood House."

"But you were in the woods the following Thursday. You said you saw Mr. Mortlake then," Thorne objected.

"I saw him come out of these woods, but I myself was on the hill opposite. I'll show you," Miss Gray volunteered.

"Thank you," Thorne said again, but this time without gratitude.

Nor was he any better pleased when they returned to the car, and Miss Gray pointed to the open hillside on the other side of the road. The effort of toiling up those undulating slopes held no attraction for him. His shoes were already filthy, the bottom of his trouser legs splashed and dirty. Grass stains would make matters worse.

"How could you be sure it was Roy Mortlake from so far away?" he asked. "You can't have known him very well, Miss Gray."

Once more Cassandra Gray was positive. "I had my field glasses, Superintendent. I almost always carry them in the country. Mr. Mortlake was an easily recognizable figure. I'll show you the exact place I was sitting and you can judge for yourself."

Hurriedly Bill Abbot, who at that point had been reading his superior's thoughts with unusual accuracy, rubbed the bottom of his nose to hide his grin. He was too slow. Thorne had noted his amusement.

The Superintendent took his revenge. He looked deliberately at his watch and said, "Sergeant Abbot will go with you. It's really only a formality, and he's as competent as I am to confirm what you say. I must get on the radio to my headquarters."

With a pleasant wave of his hand Superintendent Thorne got into the car, leaving the Sergeant to accompany Miss Gray. He found a cloth, got the worst of the dirt off his shoes and did what he could for his trousers, wondering how Cassandra Gray and Abbot had managed to negotiate the woodland track with such ease. Then he turned to his radio.

A report on the Blairs had come in from the hospital. The news was both good and bad. Maurice Blair had so far responded surprisingly well to what treatment was possible; in his case the prognosis was hopeful. Nina Blair, however, appeared to be deteriorating and her condition was critical; the chances of her survival were said to be minimal.

Another victim, thought Thorne, and another complication. There could be others. But there was no pattern to these deaths. Whichever way you looked they made no sense. Irritably Thorne thrust his head out of the car window. Two small figures, ever growing larger, were striding down the folds of the hill—Cassandra Gray and Sergeant Abbot.

Could Miss Gray conceivably be right? Thorne wondered. Was it possible that Mortlake's murder was incidental? Miranda had a great admiration for Miss Gray, and he'd learned to respect Miranda's judgement. But was this kind of subjective opinion really relevant now? There were other points to consider. If he wasted police time, and thus police money, on a wild goose chase when a perfectly adequate and chargeable suspect was available, his superiors would take a dim view. There would be a question mark on his record that might militate against promotion in the future.

George Thorne pulled at his moustache. He'd never let such considerations influence him in the past, and he was damned if he would now. Quickly he got back on his radio.

"I want everything you can get on the Hurleys and the Blairs," he said, "and I want it yesterday, not in three weeks' time. Get on to the Met and any other Force that can help. And I mean everything, however trivial, even bits of gossip. Don't be put off by their standing in their communities. If there's dirt, get it found. Fast."

Smiling benignly, Superintendent Thorne got out of the car as Miss Gray and Sergeant Abbot reached the road. He held open the door for her, and climbed in himself.

"Wychwood House, Sergeant Abbot," he said.

# Chapter 17

John and Rose Kempton were in the office at Wych-wood House, going through the cancellations and trying to calculate their probable financial position at the end of the year. Their capital was limited, and in a very few days a profitable business had been transformed into a dubious operation. Rose looked drawn and dispirited; she had noticeably lost weight in the last couple of weeks, and it didn't suit her. John was grim but determined.

"We can survive," he said. "It'll mean borrowing more from the bank, but the hotel's good collateral."

"Is it? Still?" Rose queried.

"Yes." John was firm. "The main problem's going to be cash flow. It's the same in any business that gets into deep water. As soon as it becomes known that some outfit's down on its luck, all the creditors send in their bills, want payment at once and demand cash on the nail in future. No one trusts you any more. And this compounds the difficulty and makes everything—"

He broke off as there was a tap at the door. "May I come in?" Superintendent Thorne said, already inside the room. He was at his blandest. "Ah, both of you here. Good. I'd like a chat. I hope I'm not interrupting anything vital."

"No. Sit down, George," John Kempton said resignedly. "We were just trying to work out how long we can keep Wychwood House going in the present state of affairs."

Thorne nodded his sympathy and made himself comfortable in the chair John Kempton had indicated. He said, "Am I right in thinking that hoteliers often know far more about their regular guests than those guests would credit?" He looked at Rose.

Rose hesitated. "Well, yes," she agreed finally. "Of course, some are more forthcoming than others, but they all let drop little things about themselves, and one learns to be observant—to some extent, one has to be."

Kempton was more direct. "Who are you talking about?"

"Tell me about the Hurleys first," Thorne said. "They drive a big car, come here for holidays. Does the Church of England pay its clergy that well?"

"No, I don't think so. I expect they've got private money," Kempton said. "Perhaps they inherited it. People do, you know. After all, we did—on a small scale. But I've absolutely no idea about the Hurleys."

"A lot?" Thorne asked. He wanted them to start talking, to produce titbits of gossip.

Rose was quicker than John to grasp the sort of thing that Thorne was seeking. "The Canon always does—did— himself proud," she said. "But I think that basically he was a selfish man. Neither his wife nor his daughter seem to have many luxuries. Their clothes are good and plain, but they have to last—I've seen one of Mrs. Hurley's evening dresses for at least three years. They don't have much jewellery, either. I once heard Alice Hurley admire a diamond brooch that Lady Georgina was wearing; the Canon called it an 'unnecessary piece of self-adornment.'"

"Do you think the women resented this attitude?" asked Thorne.

"No, not really. I guess they just accepted it." Rose shrugged. "What else could they do? They're both nice, but they're doormats."

"That's a pity, especially for the girl. After all, she's young and not that unattractive." Thorne did his best to speak casually; he had no wish to lead them. But his suggestion provoked no comment, and he was forced to continue. "Has Tom Latimer ever said anything about her to either of you?"

"Tom? About Alice Hurley? You mean—" Rose laughed. "Oh, George, you must be joking."

John Kempton didn't share Rose's amusement. "Why do you ask?" he demanded suspiciously.

"Oh, just a thought. And I've heard rumours. What do you know, John?"

"I don't *know* anything."

The words erupted in a burst of unexpected irritation. Thorne merely waited, and reluctantly Kempton explained how he had come upon Alice Hurley and Tom Latimer by the garages the day the Hurleys arrived. He said Latimer had been quick to tell him about a lost glove, but he'd got the impression he'd interrupted something.

"What sort of something?" prompted Thorne.

"Well, they were certainly standing pretty close to each other."

"You never mentioned this, John." Rose was surprised.

"It was just a fleeting impression. Stupid, perhaps. Not worth mentioning."

"But you remembered it," Thorne said gently.

Kempton made no reply, and Thorne let the point go. He asked them about the Winstons and the Ravens in order to conceal his real interests, then came to the Blairs. Here the Kemptons were in total agreement. Nina Blair was a trial, a demanding woman who traded on her poor health to get her own way.

"And Maurice?" asked Thorne.

"A nice chap," John said, "but another doormat, as Rose would say."

"I can't think how he ever came to marry her," Rose added. "She's years older than he is. I suppose she's quite pretty, and she's always beautifully dressed, but she must be difficult to live with. Not that I've ever heard him complain. I agree with John—he's a nice man, kind and considerate—and I suppose people adjust to each other."

"Is it his money or hers?" Thorne asked abruptly. It was nearing lunchtime, and he was beginning to feel hungry.

But this was a question the Kemptons couldn't answer. They agreed that, from what they knew of the Blairs' lifestyle, there was no shortage of money, and as far as they knew Maurice Blair didn't work. As John had said about the Hurleys, in spite of taxes there were still plenty of people around with inherited wealth.

Enough for the moment, thought Superintendent Thorne, who liked his meals at regular intervals. The Kemptons scarcely needed his hint. John would have offered him a drink at once, but Rose stopped him; George Thorne might be a friend, but right now he was on duty. Drinks and lunch, she said firmly, would be served to him—and to Sergeant Abbot if he was in the hotel—in what everyone had come to call the interview room. She smiled to take any sting out of her remarks, and promised that the meal would be up to Wychwood House standards.

Rose Kempton kept her promise. The lunch was simple but excellent, just the job for two hard-working coppers, as Sergeant Abbot remarked appreciatively. As they ate, they discussed the case and Abbot reported to his superior; the Sergeant's attention during the morning had been concentrated on Paul Kempton, and the questions he had been asking were similar to Thorne's.

The results, too, were almost identical, though Paul had taken a different view of Alice Hurley. In his opinion Alice had become less inclined to accept her dull life. On this visit, he said, Alice's tongue had been sharper than on previous occasions, and she had shown a greater determination to get her own way and follow her own inclinations. He added that he had overheard the Canon complaining that Alice had insisted on going for a walk in spite of his warning that a storm was about to break. And there had been the strange incident of the medicine bottle, reported by a maid.

"According to Paul Kempton," Sergeant Abbot said, "the girl doing the Hurleys' room had the distinct impression that Miss Hurley broke the bottle on purpose. It was in a perfectly safe place, far from the edge of the washbasin. The girl told Paul that Miss Hurley hurried into the room looking flushed and excited, said she'd come to fetch something for her mother and went into the bathroom. The crash came immediately, and Miss Hurley hurried out again with just a hasty word of explanation. But I suppose it's a big assumption that the maid's impression was right. And anyway, even if it was, why?"

"Medicine would have to be replaced," Thorne said

thoughtfully. "Maybe she wanted an excuse to visit a chemist—perhaps an opportunity to meet someone away from Wychwood House. A man, do you think? Don't forget our Mr. Latimer. There could be truth in what Mortlake told the Canon about the two of them." Thorne finished his coffee, tried the pot and found it empty. "Anyway, get rid of our trays, Sergeant Abbot, and go and fetch Miss Hurley."

The Superintendent concealed his considerable interest as he studied Alice carefully while Abbot brought her in and ensconced her in a chair across the desk. She was wearing a light blue suit, having made no attempt at the mourning which the Canon would almost certainly have deemed desirable and appropriate. Her eyes were bright and clear and showed no signs of grief. She sat straight, her hands clasped in her lap, and appeared totally composed.

Thorne began by offering her his condolences on the death of her father. Alice smiled her thanks, but said nothing. The silence lengthened as Thorne unnecessarily shuffled some papers. Then he looked up sharply.

"Miss Hurley," he said, "did you have a quarrel with your father over Tom Latimer?"

"What?" Alice drew a quick breath; it was the last question she had expected. "I—I don't know what business it—" Her lips came together in a firm line, blocking off her words. Her chin lifted. "Superintendent, the answer's no. I had no quarrel with my father over—over anything."

"All right, Miss Hurley. I'll reword my question." Thorne was not distracted by her response. "Did your father disapprove of your relationship with Mr. Latimer?"

Now Alice took her time before answering, and she spoke slowly. "The answer's again no, Superintendent, for the very simple reason that he knew nothing about it. He died before—before I had a chance to tell him. But I very much doubt if he'd have approved of my becoming Mrs. Thomas Lane-Coln. I needn't tell you why, Superintendent, need I? Though he was a clergyman, and devout, he was also narrow, full of prejudices. He'd have been ashamed to have an ex-convict as a son-in-law."

Thorne did his best to hide his surprise. He hadn't expected such a rapid agreement that a relationship existed; nor had he expected Alice Hurley to be aware of Latimer's past, nor to show such brutal frankness with regard to her father. At the side of the room Abbot coughed, as if to cover the sudden silence.

"Have I shocked you?" Alice said at last, looking from Thorne to Abbot and back again. "I'm sorry, but I've only told you the truth."

"I appreciate that, Miss Hurley. Thank you," Thorne said, wondering if her new-found self-confidence was in some sense due to Tom Latimer. "You must forgive me for asking you such personal questions. And I'm afraid there are more, now concerned with money. Your father was a rich man?"

"I'd have called him far from rich, Superintendent. It's a matter of public record that a Canon's stipend is just over nine thousand pounds a year. Would you call that rich? What rank does it compare with in the police force?"

Thorne gave no direct reply. Instead, he commented, "Canon Hurley stayed at this hotel with his family for two or three weeks, regularly. He owned an expensive car. He didn't give the impression that he was a poor man, Miss Hurley. I must assume he had another source of income."

"He had a small private income, very small, Superintendent. But my mother's brother is rich—and generous. He gave us this holiday every year at Wychwood House. We could have gone anywhere, but my father preferred this place. He also gave us the Daimler, when he bought himself a new car." She smiled wryly. "Superintendent, these are facts that my father chose to forget except when it became absolutely necessary."

"I see," said Thorne thoughtfully. "So your parents' apparent lifestyle was false, in a sense."

"If you want to put it like that, yes."

"What happens to your mother now?"

"Of her own right she'll get a pension and a small annuity. That's all. But I'm sure my uncle will help."

"Of course," repeated Thorne. "But all this means that your father's objections to your marriage plans could have made no difference to you."

"Financially, no. But I'm very fond of my mother, and it would have been an extremely difficult situation. I was hoping to—to win Father over once he realized I was determined to marry Tom."

Thorne nodded understandingly. In fact, he was considering the extent to which Tom Latimer would have trusted Alice's determination. She would have been under considerable pressure, possibly from both parents, not to marry an ex-con with no prospects. If Latimer had doubted her willpower and hadn't known about the money, he might—possibly—have seen the Canon as an obstacle to be removed. But the "ifs" would have to wait, Thorne decided; it wasn't worth raising either point with Miss Hurley.

Changing the subject, the Superintendent led her once more through the events of the Friday when Mortlake had been found dead. He learned nothing new, but he noted that Alice Hurley had relaxed. Clearly she thought the matters they were now discussing, however unpleasant, were not her personal concern.

However, when they came to the Monday and the Fowler's party she showed more interest, though she remained at ease. "My father ate very little there," she said. "He didn't like what he called bits and pieces."

"But he had some of the pastry heart," Thorne insisted.

"Yes, everyone did. You know that, Superintendent."

"Were you nearby when it was offered to him?"

It was a new question, and Alice frowned. "Yes, actually I was," she said slowly. "I remember he wanted to refuse it, but of course that wasn't possible; it was a substitute for an anniversary cake. But he insisted on swapping his piece for mine because he said mine was smaller, though I don't think it was."

Out of the corner of his eye the Superintendent saw Sergeant Abbot's head turn sharply in his direction. "You never mentioned that before, Miss Hurley," he said, keeping his voice level.

"I'm sorry. It just didn't occur to me." Alice shrugged.

And maybe I didn't ask the right question, Thorne thought. "It doesn't matter," he said. "Probably not in the least important, Miss Hurley, but every little helps—or at least we hope it does." He smiled at her benignly.

As he was to tell Miranda later, he as near as dammit left it there, thanked the Hurley girl for her cooperation and wished her good day. After all, he already knew all the details that anyone could remember of what had been eaten and drunk by individuals at the party and the dinner; he had been through them repeatedly. But something— possibly the thought that he had somehow missed a question previously—something made him raise one more query.

"I'm told that the—er—the friendly spirit of the party kind of spilled over to the dinner afterwards, if you see what I mean. Was that so, in your opinion?"

"I suppose so." Alice suppressed a sigh. She was thankful the Superintendent's questions had become so general, but she couldn't imagine where they were leading. "The tables had been rearranged, for one thing. A lot of people had left because of Mr. Mortlake's death so that only part of the dining-room was being used, and as a result the tables were closer together than usual. It made the whole thing more—more intimate."

"I see," said Thorne. "I hadn't quite realized that. Whose table was closest to yours, Miss Hurley?"

She thought for a moment. "We had the Blairs on one side and the Ravens on the other. Father didn't much like the arrangement. He got on all right with the Blairs, but he didn't approve of Polly and Vern." Alice made a wry face. "He insisted on having the seat furthest from them."

On impulse Thorne said, "Come and show me."

He was on his feet, ready to usher her from the room. Alice got up more slowly, nonplussed by the Superintendent's request. Abbot, also taken by surprise at Thorne's sudden change of tactics, hurried to open the door for them.

They went along to the dining-room in silence. Lunch had been cleared, dinner not yet laid. A maid was vacuuming the floor. Thorne gestured to her to turn off the machine and waved her away.

Alice said, "The tables have been rearranged again since Father died and the Blairs have gone to hospital. But that particular night . . ."

She took the two police officers across the room and showed them exactly where her father had been sitting, and his position in relation to the others nearby. Abbot, at Thorne's bidding, drew up chairs and placed them where Alice indicated. Thorne regarded the scene gloomily; it suggested nothing to him, and yet . . .

At last, more for the sake of something to say than because he wanted an answer, he asked, "I suppose the Blairs didn't suggest your Father should try their wine, Miss Hurley? Nothing else—er—odd happened—something trivial that no one's thought to mention?"

"No, Superintendent, I'm afraid not." Alice looked at Thorne strangely and shook her head.

"Ah, well. Thank you, Miss Hurley. You've been very patient," Thorne said, resigned to the fact that the feeling he was on to something had played him false for once.

He gestured to Alice to precede them from the room. The Sergeant followed behind. The Superintendent was losing his grip, Bill Abbot thought. What had been the point of this—this reconstruction, if you could call it that? It had been pitiful, embarrassing and completely non-productive, as was only to be expected when you knew with what painstaking care everyone's movements and intake of food on that fateful Monday had been investigated and collated.

By now they were almost at the door of the dining-room. Alice turned her head, about to say something to Thorne over her shoulder. Then she stopped dead, so that he almost bumped into her.

"Superintendent!"

"Yes, Miss Hurley." With a tremendous effort Thorne managed to keep the hope from his voice. "You've remembered something?"

"Yes. You were asking if the Blairs had offered Father wine. Well, they didn't—not wine. But we ran out of pepper at our table—the hotel staff had become a little disorganized, as was only to be expected in the circumstances—and—and Mrs. Blair gave my father their pepper-mill. I don't expect it's relevant, but . . ." She pointed to the pretty hand-painted china pepper-mills that were sitting in rows on a side table. "I remembered when I saw them. Father liked a lot of pepper, but Mother and I never take it."

George Thorne nodded. He couldn't trust himself to speak. He wanted to kiss Alice Hurley. *Amanita phalloides* ground up and added to the peppercorns in the mill on the Blairs' table, a mill shared accidentally by the Canon. The pastry heart, to use an inappropriate cliché, had been a red herring—a red herring devised by a cunning, devious murderer.

There was still a long way to go, the Superintendent reminded himself, but at last there was a chance he was on the right road.

# Chapter 18

Nina Blair died at six o'clock on Monday morning.

At nine o'clock Thorne was sitting in his Chief Constable's office. There were dark circles under the Superintendent's eyes, and his eager arguments could not conceal his underlying weariness. He had been working hard and had had very little sleep since Alice Hurley remembered Mrs. Blair lending the Canon the pepper-mill from her table at dinner after the Fowlers' party. Everything followed from that bit of evidence. Now, though his case was far from complete, he was convinced he was right. It remained to convince his superiors.

"So you believe Mrs. Blair was always the intended victim?" the Chief Constable said.

"Yes, sir." Thorne was positive. "I believe that something was added to that pastry heart so that a lot of the guests would be ill with symptoms of food poisoning. It wouldn't have been necessary to go in for anything very exotic. The experts tell me it would have been simple to give them real food poisoning. A little raw meat—frozen poultry bits from any supermarket, say—left to unfreeze in a warm, moist atmosphere would do the trick. Just leave them in a plastic bag with a little water in a sunny place, and there'd be a good chance they'd grow enough *Salmonella* to keep any collection of hotel guests up all night with diarrhœa and vomiting. Anyway, it needn't have been a gamble; you can guess the simple but pretty unpleasant means our joker could have used to make sure

152

the stuff was contaminated with something. This case is putting me right off my food," the Superintendent added.

"So?" said the Chief Constable.

"So cut the stuff up finely and sprinkle it on part of the heart. I gather the texture of the surface of the thing was something like a pizza, so that such an addition wouldn't be noticed."

"I see," said the Chief Constable. "And an epidemic of that kind would disguise from any doctor—in this case, the unfortunate Dr. Band—the fact that Mrs. Blair wasn't just suffering from food poisoning like the others."

"Exactly, sir," said Thorne. "And early diagnosis is essential if there's to be any hope of saving a victim of phalloidine poisoning. The actual Death Cap mushroom, the *Amanita phalloides*, I'm sure we'll find, was crushed up and put in the Blairs' pepper-mill. It wouldn't have taken much to do the trick, and no one would notice some white grains among the black when they were twisting the thing over their plate. Even if they did, they'd probably have thought it contained a mixture of black and white peppercorns."

"So it was pure chance that Canon Hurley died too?"

"Yes, sir. No one could have foreseen that the Hurleys' table would run out of pepper, or even if someone emptied the Canon's mill on purpose, no one could have foreseen Mrs. Blair would lend him theirs."

"Okay, I accept that. The Canon was unlucky," the Chief Constable said after a moment's thought. "But why do you choose Mrs. Blair as the intended corpse? It could just as easily have been Blair himself. After all, he was poisoned too."

"It's—possible, sir, but the method is against it. Mrs. Blair was known to use a lot of pepper. She was always talking about her time east of Suez when she was young, and how she'd grown to like curries and highly-flavoured dishes. Besides, Mr. Blair seems to be recovering; I suspect he himself took a minimal amount—if any."

The Chief Constable picked up the blue and white pepper-mill that stood on the desk between them. "Very pretty," he said. "You say these are made by a small outfit in Colombury exclusively for the hotel?"

"That's right, sir. They're not on sale to the public, though the place does get an occasional inquiry. But we checked," he added quickly. "No one's tried to buy one for at least two years."

"So the killer was probably someone on the premises, with easy access to the things." The Chief Constable spoke ruminatively. "You know, the death of Mrs. Blair *could* have been decided on after Mortlake was killed. The time gap between the two murders could be explained by the need to prepare the contaminated food and find the mushroom. In which case, you can't exclude the possibility that this Mortlake character was the intended victim. And who better than John Kempton, even if he isn't a true countryman, to be able to find the Death Cap and arrange both murders? He was on his home ground, presumably with greater local knowledge and better facilities than any of his guests. And he certainly had an excellent motive for wanting Mortlake dead."

"Sir," Superintendent Thorne acknowledged the force of the Chief Constable's argument a little stiffly.

The Chief Constable grinned at him. "No, George. I think you're right. It doesn't gel, does it? No one, having committed a simple brutal killing is going to plan an incredibly devious murder in order to cover his tracks, and I can't really visualize two completely separate murderers running around Wychwood House at the same time. So, whatever the actual sequence of events, I think we've got to assume that Mrs. Blair's death was planned before Mortlake's."

"Then you agree, sir," Thorne said quickly. "Mortlake was killed because he knew something—or saw something— that made him a danger to Mrs. Blair's murderer."

"Perhaps Mortlake saw him picking mushrooms," said the Chief Constable lightly. "And I'm not altogether joking, George. It could be. But who might want Mrs. Blair dead? That's the next question for you to tackle."

"We've already started on that aspect, sir." Thorne spoke with satisfaction, not for the first time blessing a Chief Constable who was both intelligent and understanding and was prepared to give him such a free hand. "As usual, the obvious suspect's the husband and we're taking a very careful look at him. On the face of it Maurice Blair is a pleasant, likeable chap, and a devoted husband—but who knows?"

"Let's hope we do—and before too long," said the Chief Constable. "What about the money question?"

"There's no doubt they were pretty well off, and we're doing what we can to get a grip on the details—Mrs. Blair's will and so on," said the Superintendent.

The Chief Constable gave the china pepper-mill a final inspection and then pushed it back across the desk to his Superintendent. "I suppose we'll see one of these as an exhibit at the trial—assuming you get so far," he said.

"We shall, sir," said Thorne, with conviction.

Thorne returned to his office well pleased with his progress. He was extremely thankful that, with Nina Blair established as the primary victim, the Kemptons would no longer be under suspicion. The next best thing he could do for them, he thought, was to clear up the case as soon as possible, so that it would be forgotten and the hotel would return to normality. The longer the whole sorry business dragged on the worse it would be for Wychwood House.

Bill Abbot, who had been sitting at the Superintendent's desk, leapt to his feet as Thorne came into the room. "I was answering the phone, sir. Miss Cassandra Gray rang back."

"Good. What did she have to say?"

"That she's never seen anyone other than Mr. Mortlake in or near those woods, but we might ask Mr. Blair."

"Blair? Why Blair? I assume you inquired, Sergeant."

Abbot contrived to look offended. "Of course I did, sir. What she said was that the day she saw Mortlake come out of the woods—the day the storm broke, that was—he and Mr. Blair returned to Wychwood House at the same time, both soaked. She understood they'd met while out walking."

Thorne nodded his interest at this item of information, but didn't comment. "Anything else, Sergeant?"

"Yes, sir, but not good. None of the fancy pepper-mills collected from Wychwood House show any traces of this *Amanita phalloides* stuff, according to forensic."

"Damn!" said Thorne. "Miss Hurley was positive the Canon didn't pass the Blairs' mill back to them, so it must have been on the Hurleys' table when they all moved to the lounge for coffee. I suppose anyone could have sneaked into the dining-room to collect it, but he'd have to have been pretty nippy—before the tables were cleared for cleaning and all the salts and peppers and things were moved to that side table and mixed up. It would have been difficult with the staff around."

Abbot said helpfully, "Surely, whatever happened and whoever it was, he had to be sure to find it, in case anyone else used it the next day, or later."

"I guess you're right," said Thorne slowly. "However little of the damned fungus he used to start with, our killer could never rely on it becoming sufficiently—sufficiently—diluted, if that's the word, to be safe, until the blasted mills were emptied and cleaned. I wonder how often that's done."

The Superintendent was thinking aloud, and Sergeant Abbot made no attempt to reply. There was a pause before Thorne went on. "As you say, Sergeant Abbot, someone just *had* to risk collecting it. Perhaps he'd had the sense to put a mark on it—a nick in the china or something—just in case it got moved or mixed up." He paused reflectively, then added, "That must be why forensic haven't found any traces of the stuff—the right one's gone missing. We've got to make every effort to find that pepper-mill, Sergeant—though it's probably been smashed up into small bits and buried by now. It's what we'll need to clinch things, and I doubt if the DPP'll think we've an adequate case without it."

Mrs. Dearden called to them from the reception desk as they entered the hall of Wychwood House.

"Good morning," said Thorne affably. "What can we do for you, Mrs. Dearden?"

"I wanted to ask after the Blairs."

"Mrs. Blair died about six o'clock this morning. Mr. Blair seems to be improving."

"Oh dear! Poor Mrs. Blair! I know she could be a bit of a trial sometimes, but . . ." Mrs. Dearden sounded genu

inely sorry. "Poor Mr. Blair, too. I can't think what he'll
do without her. He was always so devoted."

"In spite of her being—difficult?"

"Oh yes. He never complained. Incidentally, Superintendent, a friend of theirs telephoned to inquire after
them. She'd heard about it on the radio. I said we hadn't
any news at the moment, and suggested she phone the
hospital. But if anyone else inquires, shall I tell them
about poor Mrs. Blair?"

"Why not?" Thorne said, and added casually, "Did
this friend give any name?"

"No. I asked, but she said it didn't matter."

"Thanks." Thorne began to move away.

"Superintendent! I—" Helen Dearden make a throw-
away gesture with one hand. "I could be imagining things,
and it probably isn't in the least important, but . . ."

"Yes, Mrs. Dearden," prompted Thorne, as he turned
back.

"I told you the girl who phoned said she was a friend
of theirs, but she sounded sort of strange. Unnatural
almost—as if she was putting on an act. I got the impression there might be someone beside her prompting her
with questions." Helen Dearden stopped and laughed at
herself apologetically. "I expect you're thinking I'm a fool,
Superintendent."

"Far from it, Mrs. Dearden," Thorne replied. "This—
er—girl you're speaking of. Could you make a guess at her
age?"

"Fifteen or sixteen?" Mrs. Dearden hazarded.

Thorne thanked her again, hiding his disappointment.
It wasn't the answer he'd expected, even hoped for. He
was to be equally disappointed by Rose Kempton. The
pepper-mills were counted regularly, but there was a natural wastage, and no one could say how many had been in
use at any particular time. She agreed with his suggestion
that one could have gone missing without anyone commenting on the fact, but thought that one of the waitresses
or maids might have noticed.

Rose departed with Sergeant Abbot to make inquiries
among the staff, while the Superintendent, having ob-
tained a passkey, went up to the Blairs' room. A quick

search revealed nothing of any interest and Thorne wondered if he should have the room sealed until it could be
examined by experts. He had just decided against this
when he heard heavy footsteps in the corridor and a loud
knock on the door.

Sergeant Abbot came in, looking pleased with himself. "Traced it, sir, or I hope we have. One of the maids
says she went into the dining-room that Monday night to
start laying the next day's breakfast. She saw the young
American, Vernon Raven, by the table where the pepper-
mills were standing. She didn't actually see him nick one,
but she's pretty sure he did. Anyway, she says he was a bit
tight—most of the guests had a lot to drink that evening—
and he thrust a five-pound note in her hand, muttered
something about a souvenir and told her not to tell a soul.
Which she hasn't—not until now."

"Where are the Ravens? They've left the hotel?"

"Yes, sir. They're staying in Stratford, at the Swan."

"Okay, Sergeant Abbot. Get hold of the police there,
explain the situation and tell them we need that pepper-
mill at our headquarters as fast as it can get there. Faster,
if possible." Thorne beamed with satisfaction. "If forensic
don't find traces of *Amanita* what's-it in this mill, I'll—"
He didn't bother to complete his sentence.

That afternoon started as a trying time for George
Thorne. Pleased as he was that the missing pepper-mill
had been traced, he now worried lest Vern Raven had
washed it out for packing or, having taken it on impulse,
had subsequently thrown it away. He wouldn't be happy
till it was safely in the lab and he'd got the report.

Moreover, the interview he had hoped to conduct
with Maurice Blair at the hospital had proved impossible.
Mr. Blair, he was informed, had been extremely upset at
the death of hs wife; he had become quite hysterical and
had had to be sedated. There was no hope of seeing him
until the next morning at the earliest.

Nor was Dr. Crewe, the consultant, immediately available. It was the afternoon of his clinic and there was a long
list of patients waiting to see him. The nurse smiled blandly

at Thorne, who regarded her frostily for several seconds before he spoke.

"Would you please inform Dr. Crewe that Detective-Superintendent Thorne of the Thames Valley Police is here and urgently needs five minutes of his time," he said firmly. "At the doctor's convenience, naturally."

The nurse argued no further; she knew authority when she met it. Thorne's message was delivered and, as soon as the patient with Dr. Crewe had departed, Thorne was shown into the consulting room.

"You're busy," the Superintendent said at once, having seen the row of people sitting and waiting in the corridor outside. "I'll be brief. Mrs. Blair died of liver failure, the result of phalloidine poisoning. Am I right, doctor?"

"I wouldn't swear to it till after the PM, but it's a safe bet, yes."

"But Mr. Blair no longer shows any signs of poisoning. Does that surprise you?"

Dr. Crewe ran a hand through his red hair, and regarded the Superintendent thoughtfully. "Blair and his wife were sent here by Dr. Band because their urine samples were discoloured, and that's a fair indication of liver involvement," he said finally. "Band was absolutely right to send both of them, though later samples from Mr. Blair were normal, both in colour and in the path. lab, where they did full liver function tests immediately. And all the symptoms he complained of—cramps, nausea and so on—seem to have disappeared. I would say it's very unusual to recover so quickly from phalloidine poisoning, once having reached this secondary stage. But of course the body can play strange tricks," Crewe added.

"And that's all you can tell me?" Thorne said. "Nothing—off the record, let's say?"

"If you're thinking what I think you're thinking, Superintendent, I'll tell you what I believe. But if you quote me I'll swear you're lying." The consultant leant across his desk and fixed Thorne with his bright blue eyes. "Cramps and nausea are largely subjective symptoms, in the absence of actual vomiting, and easy to fake. And some of Mrs. Blair's urine sample could have been—spilt, shall I

say?—into Mr. Blair's, either accidentally or on purpose.
Though that depends on the circumstances in which the
samples were taken. Why don't you check with Dr. Band?
He'll know if it would have been possible."

"I will," said Thorne, "and very many thanks."

Things were improving, he thought, and when he
returned to his headquarters he found more encouragement waiting for him. The missing pepper-mill had arrived and was even now under examination. And reports
were beginning to come in from the inquiries he had
earlier set in motion about the Blairs and their circumstances. According to the Maidenhead police, there was
no doubt about their wealth, though its exact origin and
ownership were unexplained. The local solicitor who apparently dealt with some of their affairs had been interviewed and told of Mrs. Blair's death; he had promptly
telephoned the hospital. Though he rightly remained un-
willing to talk about his clients' affairs, he would be prepared to receive Detective-Superintendent Thorne, given
the Chief Constable's assurance that the inquiries were
necessary and urgent and in view of the fact that Maurice
Blair was himself unavailable.

Thorne glanced at his watch and reached for his phone.
It was too late to reach Maidenhead and tackle the solicitor that night, but there was still plenty of time for the
Chief Constable to have a few words with him and put
him on the right track. A call to Abbot made sure of
transport first thing the next morning.

Finally, to make Thorne's day complete, Dr. Band
answered his phone at once. His initial surprise at the
query gave way to interest as he described the scene in
the Blairs' bedroom last Friday morning. Clearly, thought
Thorne, the samples could easily have been mixed without
anyone's knowledge.

One of the most useful afternoons so far on this case,
Thorne said to himself as he went out to his car.

# Chapter 19

The next morning was cool and fine, but traffic was heavy and the cross-country journey to Maidenhead took Thorne and Abbot a little over an hour.

They made their number with the local Thames Valley police division, but found that the officers there had little to add to the reports they'd already transmitted to Kidlington; the only item of marginal interest was that up until two or three years ago Blair had been occasionally seen in the company of a local woman other than his wife. No one had been sufficiently inquisitive to establish the identity of the woman, and in any case there were no recent reports of their having been seen together. Nevertheless, the Superintendent showed some interest in this item; maybe it would be necessary to attempt to trace her, he thought.

Directed to the Blairs' solicitor, Thorne and Abbot found that the offices of Messrs. Larson and Larson bore no resemblance to those of the traditional country legal practice, but were housed on the fifth floor of a new office block near the centre of the town. After his conversation with the Chief Constable, Mr. Larson, the senior partner, was reasonably welcoming.

"I was terribly sorry to hear about Mrs. Blair," he began, "and all the rest of the trouble at that hotel. How is Maurice now? Not in danger, your Chief Constable told me."

"He seems to be recovering," Thorne said evenly.

"Um, yes. Well, I think I understand the situation—

and your position. And I hope you understand mine. The
Blairs have been clients of this firm for many years—ever
since they moved to this area—though we have never
dealt with all their affairs. They have London lawyers, too,
largely to deal with financial matters, I believe. But in the
circumstances we'll tell you what we can—within limits, of
course, and in confidence. I must warn you that I myself
am on the point of retirement. For some years now I've
been passing over my clients to our younger partners, and
it's my son who has been dealing with the Blairs."

"We quite understand, sir—and we're most grateful
I'm sure our questions won't embarrass your firm in any
way," Thorne said at once. "The main thing we're inter
ested in is Mrs. Blair's will. But perhaps we should be
talking to your son?"

"Unfortunately he's out of the country. I'm going to
call in Mrs. Swinson, his assistant. She's an articled clerk
and you can trust her discretion." He stretched his hand
out to his intercom, and spoke a few words. Three or four
minutes later a girl entered carrying a coffee tray. She
poured four cups, and was closely followed by a moder
ately attractive woman in her mid-thirties, with fair hair
and brown eyes. Her clothes, in Thorne's untutored opin
ion, were inexpensive, but smart and appropriate for the
office. Abbot's immediate view was that she'd look better
if she lost a little weight.

"Let me introduce Mrs. Swinson," Mr. Larson said
"Marjorie, these gentlemen are police officers—Detective
Superintendent Thorne and Sergeant Abbot. They've come
from Oxford to see us," he added helpfully.

"About—about Mr. and Mrs. Blair?" Marjorie Swinson
asked at once, without acknowledging the introductions.

"Well, let's say about *Mrs.* Blair," Larson said. "It
would hardly be right for us to discuss a living client with
the police, you know. All they want to know are the
contents of Mrs. Blair's will, and that'll be in the public
domain quite soon, I'm afraid. As I recall, it was a very
simple will for someone in her circumstances."

Mrs. Swinson didn't answer directly. Instead, she turned
to the Superintendent. "I've been reading about this awful
business—the death of Mr.—Mortlake, was it?—and the

food poisoning at that dreadful hotel. Mr. Larson told me that Mr. Blair was improving. Is that still true?"

"I understand so," replied Thorne. "I gather he's certainly out of danger."

As the Superintendent watched, Marjorie Swinson's eyes left his and she stared out of the window for a moment. Then she seemed to pull herself together and return to Larson's question.

"Very simple," she said. "Her will, I mean. She left everything to her husband. Just as he leaves—left—everything to her—" She stopped abruptly, glancing at Mr. Larson. "I'm sorry; perhaps I shouldn't have said that."

"Never mind, Marjorie," said Larson. "Blair's will is invalid now, anyway. And we can trust these officers to be discreet."

Mrs. Swinson's mind was running on other lines. "Why do the police want to know all this?" she demanded suddenly. "Mrs. Blair died from mushroom poisoning—at least according to the papers."

"Routine, madam," said Thorne, smiling persuasively. "You know as well as I do what has to happen in cases of sudden death."

"Not if they're obviously accidental."

Thorne made no comment on this remark. He turned to Larson. "Their financial affairs—you said they were handled in London. You've no idea of the size of Mrs. Blair's estate—even approximately?"

"No. And If I had I wouldn't tell you. What I will tell you is that they were well off—very well off, you've only to see their house to know that." He hesitated, glancing at Mrs. Swinson. "I think that'll be all, Marjorie," he said. "Unless you've anything else, Superintendent."

"No, no. And thank you very much for all your help. Goodbye for the present. If there are any developments I'll be in touch."

"Developments?" Marjorie Swinson was obviously reluctant to depart, but Thorne was at his blandest and swept her hesitation aside in a flurry of handshaking. Abbot got up to open the door for her.

"Sit down again," said Larson, frowning, as soon as she had gone. "Now—off the record, eh, Superintendent?"

"Off the record, sir," said Thorne promptly.

"I doubt if anyone else knows this, but over the years I've gathered that Blair was in some kind of manufacturing business and not doing too well when they married, and it was her money that set his plant on its feet. What the exact legal arrangements were I've no idea, but—" he hesitated—"*de mortuis* and all that—if I know Nina Blair she'd have tied things up neatly. As far as I know all their money matters were dealt with by their bank and its trust company—both here and in London. I'll give you the name of their local manager, but I warn you he's got an acute sense of the proprieties and he's a great friend of the Blairs. You won't get much from him without authority." He jotted a note on a piece of paper and held it out to Thorne.

The Superintendent took it, and suddenly seemed to come to a decision. He put down his coffee cup and rose to his feet, apparently now eager to end the interview and depart. "I see," he said. "There should be no difficulty about that. And thank you very much. You've been most helpful—beyond the call of duty, you might say." The solicitor unexpectedly grinned in return.

As soon as they were in the glass-fronted lobby of the building, Thorne turned to Abbot. He showed his stress and urgency by using the Sergeant's first name.

"Bill," he said, "get down to division and organize authority to interview the bank manager. Then come back and meet me in that coffee shop across the road."

"But—but we've just had coffee, sir," Abbot said unthinkingly.

"Sergeant Abbot, use your head. We may have had a stroke of luck. I want to keep an eye out for that Swinson woman. I feel in my bones she'll be useful. If I'm gone when you get back, return to the station and I'll contact you there."

Abbot gave up. "Yes, sir," he said and turned in the direction of the local police headquarters.

"More coffee?" the waitress asked.

"No, thanks."

Superintendent Thorne drew the cup, still half full of

some milky brown liquid, towards him. It was cold and unpalatable, but he forced himself to sip it—his third cup since he had come to sit in the café. He looked enviously at Sergeant Abbot, who had joined him only recently, and was still on his first.

"What if she has a sandwich at her desk and doesn't go out to lunch?" Abbot said.

"We'll give her another fifteen minutes."

Thorne stared out of the café window, willing Mrs. Marjorie Swinson to emerge from the office block opposite. He had been waiting for well over an hour; it was now a quarter past one and he was hungry and beginning to feel irritable. Abbot shifted in his seat.

Five minutes later, Mrs. Swinson came out, accompanied by an elegant woman, almost certainly a client rather than a colleague. They stood chatting on the pavement. Then they separated and Mrs. Swinson set off at a fast pace. At once Thorne threw some money on to the café table, and he and Abbot made for the door.

They caught up with her after a few yards, and walked with her, one on each side.

"Mrs. Swinson, we'd like a word with you."

"With me? What about?" Marjorie Swinson stopped in her tracks and backed defensively against the nearest shop front.

"Not in the street," Thorne said. "Perhaps we could go somewhere and have a chat."

"I'm late now and I've got to have lunch."

"Fine," said Thorne jovially. "We'll come with you. I'm hungry too."

"I just have a sandwich or a salad in the pub around the corner, and as I said I'm late. I've no time to talk."

"Mrs. Swinson, we need to talk to you. It's either over a drink and a sandwich or it's at the police station. The choice is yours."

"But why? I've done nothing wrong."

"Shall we say that we're investigating a murder, Mrs. Swinson, and we hope you'll be able to help us with our inquiries."

"Murder! You mean that man Mortlake at Wychwood House? What's that got to do with me? Or the Blairs?" she added, flushing as she took in the implications of the Superintendent's words.

She made no further attempt to argue, but led the way to the lounge bar of a modern pub. It was fairly full, but a couple were just leaving and the three of them found seats in a corner. Abbot took the orders for drinks and sandwiches.

"Tell me about yourself, Mrs. Swinson," Thorne said. "You're married. Any children?"

"Why should I—" She stared at Thorne for a moment. "Oh, very well, I've nothing to hide. I was married. Now I'm divorced. And I've a daughter."

"Aged about fifteen, shall we say?"

"Yes. How did you—"

"She telephoned Wychwood House at your prompting yesterday, to inquire after the Blairs. Didn't she, Mrs. Swinson? Or were you just interested in Maurice Blair?"

"You seem to know a lot," Mrs. Swinson said, with a bravado that was patently false. Her hand shook as she picked up her gin and tonic to take a deep drink. It seemed to give her courage, and she squared her shoulders.

Thorne seized his opportunity and changed his tactics. "Look, Mrs. Swinson," he said more gently, "why don't you tell us about it? You know in the long run we'll find out anything there is to discover—if we don't know already."

It was a moment or two before Mrs. Swinson spoke. Then, "I told you before I've done nothing wrong. It's no crime to love a man and give him a bit of comfort—certainly not when he's got a wife like Nina Blair. Maurice needs me and I need him. Larsons pay me well enough, but there's not much over for luxuries when there's two of you to live on it and no maintenance coming in from Julie's father. She's a bright girl, my Julie, and I want her to have the best . . ."

Once she began to talk, Marjorie Swinson became voluble. Words poured out, and Thorne saw no reason to doubt her sincerity. She'd had a hard life, but she'd survived, and she intended to continue surviving. She wasn't going to face trouble with the police because of Maurice Blair, fond of him as she was.

It was a simple story. She had first met Blair

Larsons' offices, with his wife. Another day she met him
in the street; he stopped and chatted. When this had
happened a couple of times she suspected that the en-
counters weren't accidental. He asked her to have a drink
with him, and she was sure they weren't. A few weeks
later she took him back to her flat, and they became
lovers.

"He's in town every Wednesday—his wife has her
hair done—and I arranged to take that afternoon off regularly. I said it was because of Julie, and worked late some
evenings to make up."

"And this started some years ago?" Thorne said.

"Almost four."

"You were content with this—this arrangement?"

"No, not really. Maurice was quite generous, but—
Actually, I was getting a bit fed up. He was always saying
he'd ask Nina for a divorce, but he never did anything
about it."

"You pressed him, Mrs. Swinson?"

"Well, yes. I had to. We could have gone on like this
for ever and—and I have another friend who wants to
marry me. He's my age and he'd be a fine father for Julie,
but he's got no money." She looked at Thorne challeng-
ingly. "Okay! I know what you're thinking. But it's not
quite like that. Remember, I'm very fond of Maurice and
I'd make him a good wife. And Julie comes first as far as
I'm concerned."

"Even if it means the death of Nina Blair?" the Superintendent asked brutally.

"For God's sake, no!" Mrs. Swinson pushed her un-
touched sandwiches away from her. "And nor would
Maurice—want that, I mean. I see what you're suggesting,
but I don't believe it. She was a bitch and she led him an
awful life, but he'd never have harmed her. He's a good,
kind man!"

"A good, kind man!" the Chief Constable repeated
twenty-four hours later. "Well, at least Blair's not short of
a character witness."

"He could get more than one if he wanted them,"
said Superintendent Thorne. "He's generally liked, sir,

though the unfortunate Mrs. Blair wasn't. But all the same he's a devious man and he's caused three deaths. Indeed, there might have been others if young Raven hadn't taken that pepper-mill as a souvenir."

"You're sure he's your man, Superintendent? You can make the case stick?"

"Yes, sir. I believe so. Once we place Nina Blair as the primary victim everything falls into place. He had the means, the opportunity and, above all, the motive to get rid of his wife. He couldn't divorce her, as he'd promised the Swinson woman. The money was all hers, though Mrs. Swinson didn't know it. According to the report from the Met, even his business was effectively run by her nominees since she'd bailed him out by buying a controlling interest when they were married; he was just a figurehead. And, without the money, his girlfriend wouldn't marry him."

"And the other deaths?"

"We've been through that, sir. I'd guess you were right and Mortlake caught him in the woods picking those damned mushrooms, and was thus a danger—particularly as he was the kind of chap who'd easily put two and two together and try a spot of blackmail. Canon Hurley was pure accident."

"Where is Blair? At the hospital?"

"No. He hired a car this morning, and was driven back to Wychwood House. We're keeping an eye on the place."

"Right. You'd better get along there then, Superintendent, and bring him in."

"Very good, sir," Thorne said.

The Superintendent returned to his own office, called Miranda to tell her he'd probably be late home, collected Sergeant Abbot and set off for Wychwood House. During the drive he tried to relax. Though he had little sympathy for Maurice Blair he wasn't looking forward to the arrest. This was a part of his job he never relished.

As far as she knew, Mr. Blair was in his room, Mrs. Dearden told them. He had arrived back at the hotel about noon, asked for a light lunch to be sent up to him and gone upstairs. "He could be having a nap now," she added. "He looked as if he needed one, poor man. Or is he expecting you, Superintendent? Was it you who phoned him just after he arrived?"

"No, not me," Thorne said. "But we'll go up."

"Phone call, sir?" Abbot queried as they got in the lift.

"Could be anyone." Thorne was terse.

Mrs. Dearden seemed to have been right. There was a "Do Not Disturb" sign on Blair's door. Thorne ignored it and knocked loudly. There was no answer and he knocked again, and banged with his fist.

"That should wake the dead, sir," Abbot said.

"Yes," Thorne said. "It should. Quick as you can, Sergeant, get a pass key. I don't like this."

Abbot ran and Thorne waited, dreading what they might find in the room. In fact, the room was empty, and a quick glance in the bathroom showed that was empty too.

Back at reception, the Superintendent demanded, "Could Mr. Blair have gone out without you seeing him?"

"Out?" said Mrs. Dearden. "I suppose so. I haven't been right here all the time, and there are always the garden doors."

"Where's his car? Still here?"

"As far as I know. Tom Latimer put it in one of the lock-ups for safety when the Blairs were taken to hospital."

Thorne hesitated for a second, then was suddenly galvanized into action. "Come on, Abbot!" he said, and ran.

As they rounded the corner of the building, they saw Latimer and Alice Hurley outside one of the overhead doors at the far end of the stable yard. Latimer held a key in his hand.

"There's an engine running in here," Latimer said anxiously as they reached him. "And the key won't work."

Thorne showed no surprise. "Then find a crowbar or something. Quick, man! Get this door open!"

Latimer, who seemed to know instinctively what was in the Superintendent's mind, was gone only a minute. Between them, he and Abbot levered at the door, which swung upwards suddenly.

A cloud of carbon monoxide billowed out from the enclosed space. The car had been backed into the garage, and it took them a moment to discern Blair's prone form lying at the far end by the car's exhaust. At once Latimer dragged a handkerchief from his pocket, wrapped it round his nose and mouth and dashed inside. As Alice screamed, he took Blair by his feet and dragged him outside into the fresher air at the side of the door.

In a moment Thorne was on his knees beside Blair. "Too late, I think," he said. "But start the mouth to mouth till we get Band and an ambulance, Sergeant. That damned Swinson woman warned him."

The noise of the engine suddenly ceased, and the Superintendent looked up to see Latimer once more emerging from the garage, this time with an envelope in his hand. "It was on the passenger seat beside him," Latimer gasped.

Thorne took it. "Well done," he said, as Alice took Tom Latimer in her arms.

Thorne was right. Blair was dead, and it was no more than he deserved. The envelope contained a full confession to three killings, but Blair made no mention of the unthinking danger to others that had resulted from his complex plot.

As usual, that night Miranda had the last words "Your ex-convict, Tom Latimer—he's not come too badly out of this, as I understand it," she remarked. "I'm very sorry for Mrs. Hurley, but without the Canon I doubt she'll object to his marrying her daughter. And I was talking to Rose Kempton. Now everything's cleared up the hotel's completely exonerated and there'll be no trial and no publicity, the bank's being helpful, and the Kemptons can see their way to a fresh start at Wychwood House."

"A happy ending?" said Thorne.